"Welcome to your new job, Ms. Lewis..."

Nikos continued, "Apparently my father has hired you to baby-sit me!"

He was obviously a madman. But he was the most stunningly handsome madman Mari had ever seen. A lesser woman—*many* lesser women—would have fallen panting at his feet.

Mari Lewis was made of sterner stuff. She had a job to fulfill, a reputation to uphold.

"Look, Mr. Costanides, I don't know why you're doing this, but—"

"You'd do better wondering why my father is doing it.... He hired you."

"To take care of his little boy."

"To take care of Nikos," her fully-grown, very masculine nemesis agreed. He poked his chest. "Me."

ANNE McALLISTER was born in California. She spent long lazy summers daydreaming on local beaches and studying surfers, swimmers and volleyball players in an effort to find the perfect hero. She finally did, not on the beach, but in a university library where she was working. She, her husband and their four children have since moved to the Midwest. She taught, copyedited, capped deodorant bottles and ghostwrote sermons before turning to her first love: writing romance fiction.

RITA Award-winning author Anne McAllister writes fast, funny and emotional romances. You'll be hooked till the very last page!

Books by Anne McAllister

Don't miss any of our special offers. Write to us at the following address for information on our newest releases.

Harlequin Reader Service
U.S.: 3010 Walden Ave., P.O. Box 1325, Buffalo, NY 14269
Canadian: P.O. Box 609, Fort Erie, Ont. L2A 5X3

ANNE McALLISTER

The Playboy and the Nanny

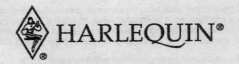

HARLEQUIN®

TORONTO • NEW YORK • LONDON
AMSTERDAM • PARIS • SYDNEY • HAMBURG
STOCKHOLM • ATHENS • TOKYO • MILAN • MADRID
PRAGUE • WARSAW • BUDAPEST • AUCKLAND

ISBN 0-373-12005-2

THE PLAYBOY AND THE NANNY

First North American Publication 1999.

Copyright © 1998 by Barbara Schenck.

Printed in U.S.A.

CHAPTER ONE

NIKOS COSTANIDES needed a woman.

Not just any woman, either. He needed a babe. Luxuriously blonde. Definitely sultry. Naturally brash. And the blowsier the better.

It wouldn't hurt if she wore a skintight leopard-spotted dress, either, he thought with a ghost of a smile. But he wasn't going to hold out for that, he decided as he tucked the telephone under his chin and punched in the number. A close approximation would do just fine.

"Debbie's Dollies Escort Service," a voice purred moments later on the other end of the line.

Nikos grinned. If the woman who came was as promising as the voice on the phone, he'd be out of here by sundown. "I'd like the services of one of your escorts this afternoon."

"Certainly, sir," the voice purred. "Whatever your heart desires."

What his heart desired was to be five thousand miles away from his father's Long Island mansion, but he knew that wasn't what the woman on the phone had in mind. Still, she would be helping him get there, so he gave the receptionist an idea of the sort of escort he wanted.

"A flagrant sort of woman?" she said doubtfully when he'd finished.

"In your face," Nikos agreed cheerfully. "Over the top. Definitely not subtle. You know what I mean?"

"Er, well," the receptionist said, though she still

5

sounded a little doubtful. Then her business sense won out. "I'm sure we have just the woman. I'll send her right out."

Nikos gave the receptionist the address. "I'm in the caretaker's cottage behind the main house. There's a party going on by the pool, but it's perfectly all right if she comes straight up the main drive and walks right past them."

Nikos looked out at the group of party-goers on the patio behind the main house—particularly at his stubborn, strait-laced father, who was carrying a footstool for Julietta, his very pregnant young wife—and flexed his shoulders in anticipation. The weight of his confinement eased slightly. It wouldn't be long now and the shackles would be completely gone.

"Yes, sir. I'll tell her. And I'm sure she'll do just what you want her to, Mr. Costanides," the receptionist assured him.

"Yes," Nikos agreed with a purr of satisfaction in his own voice. "I'm sure she will."

It was actually closer to forty-five minutes before he heard the knock on the cottage door. It was a short rap. Brisk and no-nonsense. Not especially sultry. But then it was probably hard to sound sultry in a knock.

No matter. Maybe the gardener had stopped her when she came up the drive, suspecting she was lost. She would hardly look like one of the guests coming to his stepmother's baby shower! Nikos grinned again and finished stuffing the last of his gear into a duffel bag, the better to be ready when his father threw him out.

If he'd been able to drive, he'd have been gone long before this. But a car accident following a shouting match with his father a month ago had left him with a cast on his leg that limited his mobility. It had given his father the chance he wanted—to nail Nikos down until he could badger him into working for Costanides International.

Not on your life, Nikos thought now, as he thought every time the subject came up. There would be six feet of snow in hell first.

He hauled himself out of his chair to go answer the door, thinking that if, in fact, old Thomas the gardener had stopped the floozie, it would be that much better. He would be one more person shocked by Nikos's disrespectful behavior, one more voice telling Stavros that his elder son was irredeemable, one more reason to throw the blackguard out.

To be honest, though, Nikos doubted it. After thirty years in the employment of the Costanides family, Thomas was unlikely to be shocked by anything any of them did.

It didn't matter in any case. It was his father he wanted to shock, his father he wanted to anger, not the long-suffering Thomas. It was even too bad he would horrify all those women fawning and fluttering around his gorgeous young stepmother, but that was just tough. And anyway, they'd probably love tittering and gossiping about it.

Nikos was used to being the subject of titters and gossip. He'd cultivated it once he found out how it infuriated his old man. And if people didn't have anything better to do than fret about other's supposed peccadillos, it wasn't his problem.

Still, occasional glances out the window while he'd waited for his buxom lady had proved that his audience was going to be considerably larger than he'd expected when he made the call. At least fifty of the Hamptons' best-dressed, wealthiest women were laughing and chattering on the deck around the pool as Julietta opened a pile of gaily wrapped baby gifts. Julietta's friend, Deanne, who was giving his stepmother the baby shower, must have invited the whole damn county!

Pink and blue balloons, tethered to the light poles for the occasion, bobbed in the soft summer breeze. Streamers of pink and blue ribbon fluttered from the roof of the new gazebo. He'd seen them preparing for it all morning. He'd gritted his teeth then.

Now he gritted them again as he crutched his way slowly to the door. But this time it wasn't precisely a grimace, more like a feral grin. Then, dressed only in a towel and the cast on his leg, Nikos opened the door.

She wasn't a babe.

She wasn't even blonde—or not very. Her hair was brown, but not dark, a sort of deep honey color, long and pulled back into a plait at the nape of her neck, not blowsy at all. She didn't look very sultry, either, though she had the biggest blue-green eyes he'd ever seen. Even with her big wide eyes, though, she looked prim, proper and barely more than a schoolgirl in her plain navy blue skirt and a scoop-necked shirt. It wasn't a very deeply scooped neck either, he noted with considerable irritation.

She had a good bosom on her, though, he'd give her that.

Still, if this was what Debbie's Dollies thought qualified as ''in your face,'' he didn't think they'd be in business very long. His audience was going to have to use a lot of imagination.

Nikos glanced toward the group on the deck to see if they'd even noticed her arrival, since it hadn't been nearly as spectacular as he'd hoped. Almost none of the women was paying attention.

But—Nikos smiled to himself—his father was.

The old man looked definitely curious. He stood just a little apart from the women, his body turned toward the group sitting around the table where his wife was still opening gifts. But his gaze—and his attention— were focused toward the cottage.

Good.

It would have been better, of course, if she'd been blowsy and brash, but at least she was a woman—and as such she would suffice.

Maybe her schtick was the prim schoolmarm façade that became all the more sexy by contrast once she let her hair down. Looking her over, Nikos could see where that act might have possibilities.

Too bad he wasn't going to get to test it out.

He pasted his best macho shark grin on his face. "It's about time," he reproved her, though his face spoke only eager anticipation. "But at least you got here."

She opened her mouth, but he didn't give her a chance to speak. "Come and show me what's under that prissy look, sweetheart." And, so saying, he reached out, hauled her into his arms and kissed her.

Past her ear he saw his father's jaw drop. The old man's eyes bugged. If he'd been closer, Nikos would have bet he could've seen his father's mustache quiver.

He wanted to cheer. Instead he pressed his advantage, wrapping his arms around the woman and, because upon touch she turned out to be far more tempting than he'd expected, he thrust his tongue past her parted lips as he molded her body to his.

For just a moment it was a stiff, resisting body. A

body that exactly mirrored the starchy persona she was playing.

And then, almost imperceptibly, she changed. The starch went out of her. The ice melted. She drew a sweet, astonished breath——as astonished as the one Nikos himself was drawing because, by God, yes, there was fire here!

And then she bit him!

Nikos yelped. He jerked back and swiped the side of his hand across his mouth. There was blood on it. She'd *bitten* him!

"What the hell——?" He glared at her. "You won't get very many jobs if you behave that way, lady!"

"Getting kissed like that isn't part of any job I want!"

"Kissing's extra, then?" Nikos asked, annoyed. "You'll have sex with me, but you won't kiss me?"

Her face flamed. "I'll do no such thing! What do you think——?"

"I think you're carrying the prissy librarian act too damn far!" She was going to spoil the whole thing. Nobody——least of all his father!——was going to believe he was flaunting a high-priced prostitute, if his high-priced prostitute kept on behaving like a nun.

And she didn't need to think she was going to get paid if she kept her prissiness up, either!

"Librarian act?" the woman sputtered.

"Some men might find it sexy, sweetheart. I don't." He shot a quick glance in the direction of the pool. There were several onlookers now, including his old man who was actually looking poleaxed. Maybe all was not lost.

Nikos reached out a hand and snagged hers. "Come on."

She tried to jerk away from him, twisting sideways. But clutching both crutches under one arm, he slid the other around her, making them look even cozier as he wrestled her inside.

With one leg in a cast and his arm still healing from the sprain, he was barely strong enough to hold her. And, once the door was shut and he was leaning against it, he let her go at once and shut his eyes.

Damn it! The toll of even limited exertion was still more than he could handle. He still wasn't used to it. He'd barely done more than eat, sleep and argue with his father in the two weeks he'd been out of the hospital. Damn. He hated this weakness. His head was beginning to throb again, too. It did almost every time he tried to focus on anything too long.

"What do you think you're doing?" his sexy librarian raged at him now. "Open this door. I want to leave. Now!"

"No."

Her blue-green eyes widened. "What do you mean, no?"

"Just what I said." Nikos sucked in a harsh breath. "You were hired. You're here, and by God you're going to stay. Sit down."

She didn't. She backed up. Damn it! If his father came down to see what was going on, he'd know it wasn't what Nikos wanted him to think. She was fully clothed and perfectly visible through the window.

"Damn it all. I said, sit down!" Nikos barked.

She shook her head. "I can't. I have to leave. I must have got the wrong place."

"No. It's the right place. Relax, damn it. How the hell did you get into this line of work?" he muttered.

She straightened up and glared at him. "I'm very good at my job."

She sure didn't look like it. But maybe she was—once she got out of her no-nonsense clothes.

There had sure been heat in that kiss they'd shared. It was a shame he wasn't going to be able to enjoy this encounter the way it was meant to be enjoyed.

"Well, you'll have to show me another time," he drawled.

She wrapped her arms across her breasts. "I don't intend to show you anything. I don't even know who you are! But you have to let me go!"

You have to shut up! Before his head exploded. "Sit down!" Nikos bellowed.

The force of his voice seemed to plop her right into the chair. She glared up at him.

"Not there." Nikos sighed wearily. "He can see you there. Sit on the couch."

She didn't move. "He who? What are you talking about?"

Nikos didn't answer. He just stood, teeth gritted, and looked from her to the couch expectantly. He didn't move away from the door either. Couldn't if he wanted to remain upright. God, his head hurt!

"I don't know why you're doing this," she muttered ungraciously. But at last she got up and moved to the couch.

"Thank you," Nikos said tightly. He waited until she was settled, then lowered himself gingerly into the armchair across from her. He adjusted the towel. She looked at it, the color rising in her cheeks. Quickly she glanced away, her gaze going toward the door again.

"Don't even think about it."

She looked at him, startled, but she didn't try it.

And thank God for that, because the truth was, he didn't think he had the strength to stop her.

Fortunately she didn't move. She sat right where she was, hands folded in her lap like some proper Sunday school teacher, looking at him with a combination of wariness and expectancy. There was nothing sultry or seductive about her—except the way she'd kissed him.

"You haven't been doing this long, have you?"

"Four years."

"Four years?" He couldn't imagine.

"I started while I was working on my master's degree. I have excellent qualifications. I'm very good at what I do," she told him firmly. "I have references."

Nikos bit back a grin. "I'd like to see them."

Her eyes flashed green fire at him. "I don't have to show them to the likes of you! I don't understand why you're keeping me here," she said fretfully. "I must have made a mistake and got the wrong cottage. Please! I need to talk to Mr. Costanides."

Nikos stuck his casted leg out in front of him and settled back into the chair. "You're talking to him."

"You're not Mr. Costanides! I've met Mr. Costanides! He's much older. He has a mustache. He's—"

Nikos sat bolt upright. *She'd met his father?* Bloody hell!

He couldn't believe it. The old man might have had his profligate tendencies over the years, but Nikos had never thought they'd ever extended to bringing home women of the evening! Stavros had always had too much respect for family. That was, in fact, precisely why Nikos was throwing this woman in the old man's face now.

"Who are you?" he demanded.

"My name is Mari Lewis," she said stiffly.

Which meant precisely nothing. "The dolly?" he prompted.

"Dolly?" Her brow furrowed. "No. What dolly? I'm the nanny."

The *nanny?*

Nikos gaped. And then, replaying the whole scene in his mind, he began to understand what had happened. And with understanding came not consternation, but an even greater satisfaction. An unbelievable satisfaction. The grin spread all over his face.

He'd kissed the new nanny? He'd swaggered out dressed in only a towel and, before his father's eyes, had swept his half-brother, Alex's, brand-new nanny off her feet?

No wonder the old man was looking apoplectic.

It was even better than he'd dared hope!

No matter how badly he wanted to strongarm Nikos into the company, Stavros would never let him stay here after he'd sullied darling Alexander's new nanny.

Let him stay, hell! Rigid, strait-laced Stavros would throw his philandering firstborn out on his ear!

He might even go so far as to make his secondborn his heir. And why not?

As far as Nikos could see, Alexander, the four-year-old result of his father's second marriage, was the center of the old man's universe, anyway. Alexander was the sun around which Stavros Costanides spun, the darling doted-upon child that his elder son had never been—which didn't bother Nikos a bit.

In fact it made him feel a little sorry for the kid.

Not that he'd ever had much to do with the boy. He barely even knew his half-brother. Stavros did his best to keep his younger son away from his disreputable older one.

He'd never exactly told Nikos to stay away, had never come right out and said Nikos was a bad influence on the boy, but Nikos didn't have to be told.

Nothing he did had ever pleased the old man.

He'd long ago stopped trying to. It was a hell of a lot more interesting—and rewarding—to be the thorn in Stavros Costanides's side. As long as he could leave when things got unbearable.

Since the accident Nikos hadn't been able to leave. As if the cast wasn't impediment enough, the head injury he'd received in the car accident required him to be on medication. He couldn't drive until he was through with it. And Stavros wasn't allowing anyone else to drive him.

"You're keeping me prisoner!" Nikos had accused him.

"I am looking out for your well-being," his father had replied. "Besides," he'd added scornfully, "it's not as if you have any pressing demands on your time. Work, for example?" A bitter smile had touched Stavros's features. "God forbid."

Nikos hadn't replied. There was no point. Stavros had long ago decided that he was a good-for-nothing. It was Nikos's greatest joy to do his best to confirm his father's estimation.

"It's time you settled down," his father had gone on implacably. "Until you are able to drive away under your own power, you will stay here."

And there was no arguing with him. No going around him. No convincing anybody to spirit him away. He was stuck until he could drive—with his father and his father's notion of how things ought to be done.

It was exactly what his father had been angling for. It had been the subject of their quarrel right before

Nikos's accident. It had been the subject of the quarrel they'd had last week.

Stavros had come to the cottage to try to badger Nikos into studying the company prospectus. "Learn about your inheritance," he'd demanded.

"I know all about my inheritance," Nikos had retorted bitterly, and he'd tossed the prospectus aside.

"I'll shape you up if it's the last thing I do," his father had vowed, glowering down at Nikos who had stared insolently back.

Nikos's jaw tightened. "I'd like to see you try!"

"Would you?" Stavros went very quiet. "Fine. Count on it." He'd turned on his heel and stalked out. The door shut quietly, ominously, behind him.

Nikos had ignored it, ignored *him*. He'd been enormously pleased that, for the last five days, the old man had been avoiding him completely. So he wasn't counting on Stavros being able to "shape him up."

He was counting on getting out of here—away from his father, away from all the demands and distrust, away from the bitterness and the battles and the disappointment they'd been to each other for all of Nikos's thirty-two years. He didn't need it, God knew.

Let Alex have it—all of it—and the grief that went with it.

He looked at the woman sitting primly on the sofa now. She did look like a nanny. Or a nun.

Poor Alex.

She must have impeccable credentials, Nikos thought. He paused and corrected himself—must *have had* impeccable credentials. His father wouldn't have picked anyone less worthy than Mary Poppins to look after the likes of master Alex.

"Sorry about that," he said with a repentance he didn't feel. In fact, he was still grinning.

She wasn't. "It's not funny. I have a reputation to uphold. Standards to maintain."

"I wouldn't give you a nickel for your reputation now, sweetheart," Nikos said cheerfully. "Or your standards."

"Mr. Costanides will be upset."

"I devoutly hope so." He wondered if the old man was even now bearing down on the cottage, determined to rescue Mary Poppins from his grip.

"He expected me at three. It's important for me to arrive on time," she said. "To be punctual. To be fair. To be strict. Mr. Costanides says his son needs that."

Did he? Nikos didn't know Alex well enough to say. Certainly the kid wasn't as headstrong as he'd been.

"Punctual. Fair. Strict. You must be a regular paragon. I'm sure you'll impress the hell out of him," he said lazily. "What other virtues do you have?"

"I don't use profanity," she said.

Ah, so she could sting when she wanted to. Nikos grinned. "Little brat getting out of hand? Don't want him turning out like his big brother, do we?"

The nanny looked perplexed. "Big brother? Are there *two* children? Mr. Costanides didn't mention a brother."

"I'm not surprised," Nikos said drily.

"But, yes," Miss Mari Lewis went on quite sincerely, "he did say Nikos had been giving him some problems."

"*What?*"

His yelp caused her to jump. But instead of answering him, she folded her hands in her lap, pressed her lips together, and looked like he'd have to torture the information out of her.

"What did you say?" Nikos demanded again.

She gave a quick determined shake of her head. "I shouldn't have said anything. Not about the child—or his behavior. It's indiscreet. Improper. It's entirely between me and my employer."

But Nikos wasn't listening to her babbling. "The boy," he demanded, hobbling close, glowering down at her. "What did you call him?"

Mari Lewis blinked at him like some near-sighted owl, but he wasn't ruffling her feathers. She lifted her chin, as if to tell him he wasn't going to intimidate her. Then, "Nikos," she said, exactly as he'd thought she had.

His teeth came together with a snap. "No."

"Yes."

"No," he said again. "His name is Alexander."

"No," she replied just as firmly, "it's not."

She reached down and picked her bag up and pulled out a contract. She held it out toward him. "See for yourself. It says right there. His name is Nikos. I might have got the wrong cottage, but I have not got the wrong child!"

Yes, she damned well had!

But, from his father's standpoint, obviously, no, she had not.

The old man hadn't been apoplectic at all. He might have been a little astonished when Nikos had hauled Mary Poppins into his arms and kissed her, but ultimately he would have been amused—and justified.

His son's flagrant disregard for propriety, his inappropriate kissing of a total stranger would have only underscored Stavros's notion that he had done the right thing.

The old rogue had hired a nanny to straighten him out!

Far from running down here to rescue her, the old man was probably standing up on the deck now, congratulating himself—and laughing his fool head off.

Nikos's teeth came together with a snap. His headache returned with a vengeance. He dropped his head back and shut his eyes, his mind whirling furiously. And furious was the operative word.

"I'll shape you up if it's the last thing I do." His father's words came back to haunt him. To mock him. To humiliate him.

It was Stavros Costanides, down to the ground.

"Mr....er...I'm sorry, I don't know your name—" the very proper nanny's voice broke into his bitter reverie "—but you really do have to let me go. I have to find the right cottage. I have to—"

Nikos opened his eyes and glared at her.

She blinked again, but met his gaze determinedly.

Just how determined was she? He couldn't imagine. He could bet, though. And he was willing to bet he could run her off in less than twenty-four hours.

A corner of his mouth tipped up slightly. Did the old man think he was just going to roll over and give up his wicked ways without a fight?

Well, if he did, he'd vastly underestimated his older son.

Whatever he was paying Miss Mari Lewis, it had better be a bundle. She was damned well going to earn it.

"You don't have the wrong cottage," Nikos told her.

"But you said—" She looked around, puzzled. "But...where's Nikos?"

He smiled. It was a hard smile. There was nothing pleasant about it. "I'm Nikos."

She gaped at him.

"Welcome to your new job, Ms. Lewis. Apparently my father has hired you to babysit me."

He was obviously a madman.

But he was the most stunningly handsome madman she'd ever seen. He had dark brown eyes and tousled black hair, a lean face with high cheekbones and a wicked-looking dimple just to one side of his mouth that deepened when he gave her that bitter smile of his.

And he kissed like—

Mari didn't want to think about what he kissed like! She'd never been kissed like that in her life!

A lesser woman—*many* lesser women, she was sure— would have fallen panting at his feet.

Mari Lewis was made of sterner stuff.

She had a job to fulfill, a reputation to uphold, a magazine ad and article to live up to, and a pair of lovable, impractical, dangerously gullible aunts to support.

And despite the fact that her heart was still hammering and her head was still spinning and her lips were still tingling, she needed to find Stavros Costanides. And she needed to do it fast.

But how? When Mr. Whoever-he-was was sitting next to the door, looking as if he would pounce on her if she made a move in that direction.

"Look, Mr...." She paused.

"Costanides," he said helpfully. He smiled again. The same humorless smile he'd smiled before. However heart-stopping it was, his smile wasn't meant to be friendly. It wasn't even, she was fairly sure, meant to be attractive. Unfortunately it was. The dimple deepened again.

She wanted to touch it. To touch him. Again. *Help!*

Determinedly Mari looked away and forced herself to say in a level tone, "Mr. Costanides, then. I don't know why you're doing this, but—"

"You'd do better wondering why my father is doing this."

"Your father?"

"The well-known despot, Stavros Costanides. You know? Older than me. Mustache." He parroted back her description. "The man who hired you."

"To take care of his little boy."

"To take care of Nikos," her fully-grown, very masculine nemesis agreed. He poked his chest. "Me."

"But that's ridiculous!"

"You're telling me," he muttered. His smile faded and suddenly he rubbed fiercely at his forehead. "Damn."

Mari frowned. Maybe he wasn't totally mad, after all, she thought. Maybe he was suffering from concussion— a head injury that made him think he was someone else. He certainly looked as if he'd recently done battle with something formidable—and lost.

His left leg was in a cast; he held one arm close to his body, as if he was protecting his ribs; he had a fresh scar on his jaw, and his very handsome face still showed the lingering signs of bruising beneath the left eye and temple.

"Are you all right?" she asked quickly.

He lifted his gaze to meet hers. "Would you be?"

The very bleakness of his tone startled her. It also stopped her cold, having the effect that his words hadn't had. It made her think that he wasn't talking only about his physical condition at all.

It made her worry that he might be telling her the

truth. Mari swallowed. Pushed the notion away. Tried not to think about it.

Stavros Costanides had hired her to be a nanny to his son. His little boy! She knew he had a little boy. She'd glimpsed a picture of him on the credenza in Stavros's office.

"Is that Nikos?" she'd asked him.

He'd smiled a proud papa smile and had picked up the picture, saying proudly, "That's my son."

Nikos, she'd thought.

But he hadn't actually said, "That's my son, Nikos," she realized now. He'd just agreed, "That's my son."

And the devilishly handsome man sitting across from her now was...?

"You're Nikos?" she asked faintly. "You're not... kidding?"

Deep brown eyes met hers. Slowly he shook his head. "I'm not kidding."

Outside in the distance Mari could hear the gabble of cheerful women. Overhead a jet engine droned. A bird twittered.

"But...but it doesn't make sense. I mean, why would he—?" she faltered. "You're not—" She broke off. "I understood he had a four-year-old. He showed me a picture of a four-year-old!" She gave him an accusing look.

"He does have a four-year-old. My half-brother. Alexander."

"Then it's obviously a mistake."

"It's not a mistake."

"But—"

"It's his way of making a point. He thinks I'm wasting my life. He thinks I don't take things seriously enough, that I haven't accepted my responsibilities as heir to his damned empire, that I'm shirking my duty to follow in his footsteps as the eldest son.'' His tone became more and more bitter as he spoke. His dark eyes flashed, and it was all Mari could do not to flinch under his gaze.

She didn't, because as a nanny she knew that the slightest crack in her armor could do her in. *Don't let them intimidate you,* was the cardinal rule of dealing with one's charges.

One of her charges?

She wasn't seriously thinking she was this man's nanny, was she?

It was a joke. Any minute now Stavros Costanides would come along to say he'd made his point and they would all laugh about it—though this particular son might laugh a little harshly—and then she would get her real job as nanny to Alexander.

Wouldn't she?

Oh, heavens, she'd better! She *had* to have a job. She couldn't *not* have a job!

Aunt Emmaline and Aunt Bett would be out on the street if she didn't keep this job. It had been a godsend when Stavros Costanides had called her two days ago and wanted to hire her.

"I read about you in a magazine my wife gets," he told her. "You're the woman who could make Little Lord Fauntleroy out of a Katzenjammer Kid?"

Mari remembered laughing a little self-consciously. "The writer might have been exaggerating a little," she allowed, recalling the article that had appeared in last month's issue of an upscale magazine for parents. The article had been subtitled *"Mari's not Mary, But This Nanny Could Make That Poppins Woman Take a Back*

Seat'' and it raved about Mari's ability to deal with problem kids. "I was nanny to her nephew for two years."

"He was a handful?"

"Oh, yes."

"My son is, too."

His four-year-old, she'd thought.

The more fool she.

It certainly explained the bonus offer he'd made her when she'd met him at his office yesterday afternoon. He'd detailed his son's stubbornness, his reluctance to toe the line, his determined rebellion in the face of parental authority.

"I thought I could handle it myself," he'd said gruffly. "Now I don't think so. But I need it done. If you bring him up to scratch at the end of six months— if you *last* six months—I'll give you a hundred thousand dollars bonus."

Mari had gaped at him.

And then, steepling his hands on his desk, and looking at her over the tops of his fingers, he'd said, "And if you quit before six months are up, you owe me ten."

"Ten?"

"Thousand dollars."

To him it was chicken feed. To her, in her family's straitened circumstances, it was more than she could promise.

But she wouldn't *have* to give him ten thousand dollars, she'd reminded herself—if she didn't quit. She wouldn't quit. She knew she *couldn't* quit!

"All right," she'd agreed.

"He must have been kidding," she said hopefully now to the dark brooding man who sat and watched as all these thoughts flitted across her face.

Slowly, deliberately, Nikos Costanides shook his head. "No."

"But—"

"He's hired you to reform me."

Mari wanted to deny it. She couldn't. She had the awful sinking feeling that it was true.

"I can't—"

"You bet your sweet tail you can't!" he said harshly. "So just march yourself up to the house and tell him the joke is on him."

"What do you mean?"

"I mean, go tell him you're not going to play. That whatever he's paying you, it's not enough. That there's no way on earth he can con you into staying."

Ah, but there was. There was that enormous white elephant of a house her aunts owned—their pride and joy, their legacy from their profligate father. It ate money. They couldn't give it up.

"Where would we go, dear?" Aunt Em's frail voice echoed in her ears. "We've always lived here."

"Can't put Em in one of those homes," Aunt Bett said over and over. "It'd kill her."

Probably, Mari acknowledged, it would. Aunt Em had a bad heart. It wouldn't feel any better if she learned about Aunt Bett's disastrous attempt to bail them out by playing the ponies, either.

Actually having to leave their home would likely kill them both. And Mari could see that they didn't have to leave it—she could even see that the gambling debt was paid and the house had new struts, new paint and a new roof—*if* she managed to keep this job and earn Stavros Costanides' bonus.

"No," she said. "I can't."

Nikos Costanides scowled at her. "Why the hell not?"

"Because I need the job."

"What did he offer you?"

Mari blinked. "What?"

"Obviously he offered you a bundle," Nikos said impatiently. "Fine. I'll offer you more to leave."

It was tempting. Terribly tempting. She wanted to take it. And yet—

She shook her head. "I can't."

He glared at her. "What do you mean, you can't?"

She knotted her fingers. "My reputation is at stake."

"What?" He looked thunderous.

"I have a professional reputation, as I said before." She felt her cheeks warm and, certain that he could see how flimsy that excuse was, she felt compelled to add, "Not the sort you imagined, but such as it is, it's important to me."

His jaw clenched. Their eyes battled.

Mari's heart beat faster, her pulses raced. She felt like a racehorse in the home stretch, given its head. "All you have to do is shape up," she reminded him a little breathlessly.

"Like hell. I'll be damned if I'll knuckle under to his threats!"

"Yes, well—" She took a careful shallow breath, then shrugged lightly. "Maybe you can't."

A nerve in his temple pulsed. He shoved a hand through disheveled dark hair. His eyes narrowed. "You're saying you're staying, Ms. Lewis?"

Say no, she told herself. *Walk out. To hell with your reputation, your aunts, the hundred thousand dollars, the way he kisses! Where's your common sense?*

She didn't know. She only knew that something had

happened when Nikos Costanides kissed her. She had been kissed before. Heavens, she'd even been *engaged* before. But when Ward had kissed her it had been pleasant, warm, and in a few seconds, gone.

Even now the imprint of Nikos's mouth was still on hers. The taste of him was a part of her, reaching into her. And somewhere deep inside it was as if a fundamental answering chord responded.

She hadn't known such a response existed. She wanted desperately—perhaps foolishly—to know more.

Sanity—despite her reputation, her aunts, the money—told her to say no. It was foolish. It was insane to agree to be nanny to a grown man for any reason or any amount of money.

Mari was practical. Mari was sensible. Mari was grounded.

"People who are grounded have never flown," her free spirit uncle Arthur always said with a twinkle and a hint of challenge in his eye.

She took a deep breath and said, "Yes."

CHAPTER TWO

SHE had lost her mind.

A twenty-nine-year-old virgin who'd never felt the slightest tingle—not even from the kiss of the man she'd been engaged to for three years—had no business taking on a man who looked like he ate nuns for breakfast!

But she'd committed herself.

Mari didn't see that she had any choice.

It wasn't just the fact that she'd given her word—even if Stavros Costanides had fudged a little bit on his. It wasn't just that it was a matter of honor. And pride. And integrity. And the fact that she *was* good at what she did.

It was that recently she'd felt incomplete. Unfinished. Inadequate somehow.

At least Ward had certainly thought she was!

"You want to know why I'm breaking it off?" her fiancé Ward Bishop had said last month when he'd come to tell her he'd had second thoughts about marrying her. "It's because you're a cold fish, Mari. I want to make love and you talk about the weather. I touch your breasts and you grab my hands. I kiss you and you don't respond."

"You mean I don't tear your clothes off—or mine," Mari had retorted scathingly, hurt beyond reason at her fiancé's outspoken words.

"You don't even unbutton them," Ward snarled.

Later he'd apologized, had said he'd never meant to be so blunt. "You're a fine person, Mari," he'd said in a conciliatory, unctuous manner that made her want to wipe the floor with him. "It's not your fault. You just aren't...passionate."

"I don't remember *you* burning down any buildings either!" Mari retorted, stung.

"Not with you I haven't," he'd agreed readily enough. Which she supposed meant that he and the new love of his life, Shelley—the twenty-three-year-old he was dumping her for—were setting whole forests on fire!

Well, fine. Let him. Let him have Shelley! Let them burn up the world!

She didn't care. Much.

But, as little as she wanted to admit it, long after Ward had gone his accusation still hurt. It hurt thinking there was something wrong with her, that other people had something she was lacking, some fire deep within that God had apparently forgotten to build.

And then this afternoon, completely unexpectedly, totally out of the blue, something had happened—something deep, strong, *passionate*. And all she could think was that God apparently hadn't forgotten to build the fire at all.

It just wasn't Ward who'd been given the match!

But...*Nikos Costanides?* A—

"How old are you?" she asked a glaring Nikos as she came back into the cottage with her luggage.

"Thirty-two," he growled as he watched her come in with her luggage.

A thirty-two-year-old Greek playboy? Because she had no doubt now that a mindless frivolous playboy was exactly what he was.

Mari shook her head. What *could* God have been thinking about?

Nikos apparently wondered the same thing. He was

sitting right where she had left him, scowling at her. While she'd been out finding Thomas the gardener, he had put on a pair of white shorts, and she supposed that was some concession. Still, he looked very adult, very masculine and very intimidating as he again sprawled bare-chested in the chair, watching like a sulky child as Thomas, laden down with suitcases, followed her in.

"How old are you?" he asked insolently.

She lifted her chin. "Twenty-nine."

"You don't kiss like you're twenty-nine."

Mari felt her cheeks flush. The feelings of inadequacy reared their head again. She wondered if that meant Nikos hadn't felt what she'd felt.

At his impertinent words Thomas made a disapproving noise in his throat, and Mari knew she should be feeling more embarrassed than she was, but in fact she was mostly curious. *Hadn't he?* She looked at Nikos closely.

Immediately his gaze shifted away.

Yes! He *had* felt it! Mari felt a twinge of triumph. Hugging herself inwardly, inadequacy vanquished for the moment, Mari said to Thomas as blithely as she could manage, "Don't mind him. He's just sulking."

"I am *not* sulking!"

His outrage made Mari hide another smile. "You can take them through here," she said to Thomas, ignoring Nikos. She started toward the hallway that led away from the small living room, then looked back. "I presume that's where the bedrooms are?" she said over her shoulder.

Nikos grunted something. His dark gaze was brooding as he looked at her again.

"*Did* he kiss you, miss?" Thomas asked worriedly.

"Oh, yes." She tried to sound blithe, matter-of-fact

and indifferent, not at all as if, by doing so, he had turned her world upside down.

"She's not any good at it," Nikos said loudly.

"I can see why your father thinks you need a nanny," Mari said pleasantly. "Someone needs to teach you how to behave."

Then she sailed out of the room and down the hallway. A strategic exit after having the last word was always a nanny's strength.

"A nanny?" Thomas's eyes goggled.

"Mr. Costanides has a strange sense of humor apparently," Mari said. It was all she was going to say.

"Didn't know he *had* a sense of humor," Thomas mumbled. Then, "Which room, miss?"

Behind her Nikos called, "She can sleep with me."

"Mr. Nikos!" Thomas was clearly scandalized.

"She loves it when I talk dirty." Nikos's voice followed them.

Thomas sputtered.

"Children act up when they think we're watching, Thomas," she said firmly. "I advise you to ignore him. Come along. I'll find my own room."

Down the short hallway beyond the small living room and kitchen, Mari found three bedrooms. The biggest, with a view overlooking the garden, was clearly the one Nikos was inhabiting. The king-size bed was unmade. There was a laptop computer and a lot of boating magazines scattered on the desk. *The better to choose his next yacht from*, Mari thought.

The room itself was actually very Spartan-looking, done in whites and tans and browns with just a hint of black. Somber. Harsh.

Rather like its occupant, Mari thought.

"Like my bed?" Nikos called. "It's plenty big enough to share."

She ignored him. She tried to ignore the bed, too. But the thought of sharing it with Nikos was astonishingly vivid. She could imagine him naked against those white sheets, could envision herself, equally naked, tangling with him—

Oh, girl, stop this! She'd never had such blatant fantasies in her life!

She wondered if it had something to do with the squid her Aunt Em had fixed for lunch. Was squid an aphrodisiac?

She turned and hurried out of the room.

The bedroom across from Nikos's was equipped as an office, but with a daybed instead of a sofa or pair of chairs. It didn't look as if anyone was using it at the moment. No big surprise there. If Stavros imagined that Nikos needed "shaping up," it wouldn't be because he was a workaholic!

She could have stayed in this room, but somehow Mari didn't want to be that close to Nikos Costanides— whether because she thought he might get the wrong idea, or whether she didn't trust herself, she wasn't sure.

Fortunately there was a third bedroom along the back of the house. It was a long narrow room that seemed to have been converted from a sleeping porch and was more casually decorated than the rest of the house. Airy and sunlit, with balloon curtains done in white eyelet, it was soft and romantic. Soothing, not passionate.

Just as well, Mari thought. She was curious. Not suicidal.

"Put my things here, will you, Thomas?" She went over to the window and looked out. Beyond the main house she could see the beginning of the dunes that dipped toward the Atlantic. Now, in the silence, she could hear the sounds of the waves.

"Miss?"

She turned to see that Thomas had set down her cases and now stood looking at her. He had a slight smile on his face. "I just wanted you to know, miss...he isn't as bad as he says."

"He couldn't be," Mari agreed drily.

Thomas's bare hint of a smile turned into a real one. He almost chuckled. "He'll try, though."

"It...should be interesting," Mari agreed. "Tell me, Thomas. Did you know about this? That Mr. Costanides was setting us up, I mean?"

Thomas hesitated a moment, then said, "No, but, I'm not surprised. It's no secret Mr. Costanides is worried—about Mr. Nikos, about the future of his company. He's getting older. He's had one heart attack. He wants time with Mrs. Costanides and the children. So he wants Mr. Nikos to take over. But," he added, "only if he does it the way Mr. Costanides wants."

Which was the situation in a nutshell. "And why am I sure that Nikos has his own mind?" she asked wryly.

Thomas smiled again. "Because he's his father's son." Thomas shook his head. "Mr. Costanides doesn't always handle Mr. Nikos very well."

"And he thought hiring a *nanny* would help?"

"I'm not sure he thinks anything will help at this point," Thomas said bluntly. "But this, at least, he hasn't tried."

That would make two of them.

"He won't hurt you, miss," Thomas said quickly. "He teases, that's all. If he gives you trouble, you call me. I'll come whip him into shape for you." He grinned. "Mr. Nikos listens to me."

"But not to his father." It wasn't a question.

Thomas shook his head adamantly. "Never. Mr. Costanides never talks to Mr. Nikos, come to that. Just yells. And demands." He gave a shake of his head, then brightened and looked at her. "You can fix that."

"Sounds like it's been broken for a very long time."

Thomas hesitated, then gave a small nod. "They're good men, though. Both of them."

"Then what's the problem? *Why* don't they listen to each other? *Why* don't they talk to each other?" She needed a place to start. Some clue as to what dynamic existed between them.

Thomas lifted broad shoulders. "You got to ask Mr. Nikos or Mr. Costanides about that." His warm brown eyes met hers. He reached out a hand and squeezed hers briefly. "I wish you luck, miss."

Mari thought she was going to need it.

The knock on the door was quick and staccato. Seven taps, the last two separated from the first ones in brisk, cheerful fashion.

Obviously the old man—pleased with himself and coming to gloat.

"Door's open," Nikos growled.

A second later it was, and a seductively stacked blonde in a revealing leopard-spotted dress sashayed in. "Nikos?" she purred, her eyes lighting up at the sight of him.

Oh, hell. He'd forgotten about her!

But a second later he grinned with unholy glee at the thought of what his father must be thinking now—and how gloriously shockable the Mary Poppins clone was going to be!

He pushed himself forward in the chair and held out a hand. "Come here, sweetheart," he drawled.

Debbie's Dolly shut the door behind her, then moved toward him, unbuttoning the top two buttons of her very low-cut blouse as she came. "Aw, did you hurt yourself, darlin'?" she murmured, taking in the yellowing bruises on his face. "Let me kiss it and make it better." She bent over him, giving him a good glimpse of a pair of her more outstanding assets as she did so.

"I wouldn't if I were you," said a firm female voice from the hallway.

The blonde jerked back.

Mari Lewis stood in the doorway to the living room, a stern look in her eyes. The blonde, eyes like saucers, looked quickly from Mari to him.

Nikos didn't move, just watched, fascinated, as Mari gave the blonde what looked like an affable smile, and said almost pleasantly, "Or what happened to him could happen to you."

The blonde looked beyond Nikos's bruises to his taped ribs and casted leg and gulped. Then her eyes narrowed. "Who are you?"

"His nanny."

"What?"

"I'm Nikos's nanny." Mari Lewis repeated the words as if they made perfect sense, and she said them with such forcefulness that Nikos found himself admiring her. For a second.

Right before annoyance set in.

He could sense the blonde beginning to retreat. "Don't mind her," he said, reaching out a hand and snagging hers, drawing her close. "Ms. Lewis is just a frustrated spinster my father's wished on me. She won't bother us."

"Won't I?" Mari said, and once again, though her expression was perfectly pleasant, her tone was like steel.

He didn't think it was a question even though it sounded like it. But he was damned if he was going to let some governess bully him!

"Of course not," he said. "Because if you leave," he told the blonde, though he slanted a gaze Mari's way, "she knows I'll have to kiss her again instead."

"Again?" the blonde echoed nervously. She tugged her hand out of his and stepped back, looking from Nikos to Mari, an increasingly worried expression on her face. "I...think maybe you should settle this between yourselves," she said quickly, edging toward the door.

"Excellent idea," Mari said, moving toward her.

"Terrible idea," Nikos disagreed. Didn't Debbie's Dollies have any backbone? "Come back here."

"Keep right on going," Mari suggested, herding the blonde ahead like a sheepdog nipping at the heels of a ewe. "Thomas, would you show Miss...Miss...?"

"Truffles," the blonde supplied nervously.

"Would you show Miss...Truffles the way out, please?" Mari said quite pleasantly, though Nikos was sure he could hear a hint of a smile when she said the ridiculous name. He gritted his teeth. Surely even a blonde with very little brain could have thought of a better moniker than that!

"And give her something for coming all this way," Mari added.

"You stay right here," Nikos commanded. But the blonde wasn't listening to him. She fumbled to open the door. Mari opened it for her.

"He doesn't need to give me anything. We have his credit card number," the blonde said nervously.

"You're not charging me! You didn't do any—"

"We're supposed to charge whether or not they—" Truffles-the-blonde apologized to Mari. She wasn't even looking at him! "For the, um, er...house-call, y'know?" she said a little desperately.

"Of course." Mari nodded sagely. "Makes perfect sense."

"The hell it does!" Nikos shoved himself up, trying to get out of the chair. "You can't give my money away like that!"

She turned and gave him a blithe smile. "I didn't. You did."

"Come along, miss," Thomas said smoothly, taking the blonde by the arm. He gave Nikos a hard level look over his shoulder and a slow despairing shake of his head as he steered the woman down the path. "You should be ashamed of yourself."

Nikos wasn't sure if Thomas meant the blonde or him, but judging from the look on the old gardener's face he had a pretty good idea.

The door shut. The silence was deafening.

Used to prevailing in arguments about bedtime, homework and when to allow a friend to sleep over, Mari found it a little difficult to pretend that she commonly vanquished women of the evening—as Aunt Bett called them—in the course of her work.

It's not much different than a sleepover, she told herself firmly, then rolled her eyes.

Surreptitiously she wiped damp palms on the sides of her navy skirt and drew several steadying breaths before she shut the door after Thomas and Miss—she still smiled as she thought the name—*Truffles*, and turned to face the ire of Nikos Costanides head on.

Big mistake.

The sizzle she'd felt from his kiss seemed to arc right across the room and hit her between the eyes. He was slumped back into his chair again, glaring at her, looking for all the world like a sulky child who'd just had his treat taken away, and she could feel her palms dampen and her mouth dry out. There was some deep primitive response going on inside her, too, that she didn't really want to focus on.

'Hormones, dear,' her Aunt Bett would have said, as if it was the most natural thing in the world. And doubtless Uncle Arthur would have winked at her.

Well, now was *not* the time for hormones!

No matter how curious she was, she couldn't simply jump a man she didn't know. A man she probably didn't even *want* to know!

What, she wondered, were you supposed to do if these suddenly wide-awake and raring-to-go hormones aimed you at entirely the *wrong* man?

Go slow, she cautioned herself. *Learn as much as you can about the phenomenon.* Then, once she understood it better, she could transfer the feeling to someone more suitable than Nikos Costanides.

Right now the thought of what he and Miss Truffles would be doing if she *hadn't* arrived set a blush on Mari's cheeks. Was that why he'd been so eager? she wondered with sudden dismay. Had he been primed for any woman, and simply let it all out for her?

Now there was food for thought.

She slanted a glance at him again, wondering just what sort of man he was. Surely he didn't routinely hire "women of the evening" and parade them past his father and family!

If he did, it was no wonder his father was out of patience with him.

"You don't look like you'd have to hire that sort of thing," she said now.

Nikos blinked. Then, "I don't," he said flatly.

"Then why—?"

He plucked irritably at the fabric on the arm of the chair. "Think about it," he growled at last.

Mari tried. She thought about everything that had happened since she'd knocked on the door, expecting Stavros Costanides and his four-year-old son and getting a virile man clad only in a bath towel instead. A virile man in a bath towel who'd said, "About time," and then hauled her into his arms and *kissed* her!

She hurried past that part of the memory before it could affect her equilibrium again. But as soon as she did, she had to back up and go over it again, because somehow she suspected it was the key.

Obviously he'd mistaken her for Miss Truffles. But why was he waiting to *kiss* Miss Truffles? It wasn't as if he knew the woman, for heaven's sake!

Mari was sure he'd never seen her before in his life. Anyway, even in Mari's non-existent experience, a man didn't lie in wait to kiss a woman he hired by the hour.

Unless, perhaps, he was doing it for effect.

Effect. On whom?

She remembered the gathering at the poolside. There had been a lot of women, a few children. And his father.

She remembered seeing him there, starting to go over to talk to him, but then him shaking his head and waving her on. Waiting. Watching.

For Nikos to open the door. To meet his *nanny*. To blow sky-high?

Perhaps. Or maybe to be amenable then to another

"discussion" with his father. Yes, she was willing to believe that was what Stavros had been doing.

And Nikos?

She suspected that, for all their differences, he was his father's son.

"What were you trying to prove?" she asked.

"I wasn't trying to prove anything. I was trying to get him to damned well throw me out!"

"Ah." *Flaunt the hooker in front of the family and watch Daddy take action.* She understood now. But... "He's keeping you prisoner?"

Nikos lifted the cast. "I can't drive. As soon as I can, I'm out of here."

"I see." She did. Sort of. She wondered what Stavros was playing at, hiring her, then. Nikos was certainly not going to be wearing the cast another six months.

"I doubt it," he said flatly. "He's a manipulator."

"And you're not?"

He frowned. "I'm only doing this in response to what he's done. He doesn't have to keep me here."

"He started it, in other words?"

The frown deepened. "You make it sound like two little kids fighting."

"I see some similarity," Mari pointed out.

"You don't see a damn thing."

"Well, I'm sure you'll enlighten me."

"I don't want anything to do with you."

Mari wasn't entirely sure she wanted anything to do with him, either. If she hadn't felt what she'd felt when they'd kissed, she would have been running the other way.

"Why are you staying?" Nikos demanded.

"I gave my word."

"He as much as lied to you!"

"I know that." Mari shrugged. "I'm not going to play on his level."

"You're going to reform me instead?" he said cynically.

I wish, Mari thought. She ran her tongue over her lips. "I'm going to stay here because that's what I've been hired to do. I'm going to try to help because that's my job. What happens between your father and you—well, I'll do my best."

"It won't be good enough," Nikos said. Then almost to himself he added, "It never is."

Mari, caught by his words, wanted to ask what he meant, but he hauled himself to his feet and crutched past her toward his bedroom. "I have a headache. I'm going to sleep. Do whatever the hell you want. Just go away and leave me alone."

She left him alone.

She went looking for his father. She had plenty of questions that only Stavros Costanides could answer.

He wasn't with his wife and her shower guests. Julietta waved a hand toward the house. "He took Alex in a little while ago. He's probably in his office by now. It's on the second floor. Go right on up. I think he's expecting you." As she said this last with a completely straight face, Mari merely thanked her and headed toward the house.

"'I think he's expecting you'," she muttered under her breath. "I'll bet."

Stavros was sitting at his desk, the phone to his ear, when she appeared in the doorway. When he saw her, he smiled and beckoned her in.

Mari didn't smile back. She entered the office, but she didn't take the seat he indicated. She had no intention of sitting down and putting herself at an even greater disadvantage.

"Tell Adrianos to get right on it," Stavros said into the phone. "That's right. As quick as he can." This last was almost a bark. Then he hung up and turned a thousand-watt smile on her. "Ah, Miss Lewis, you've come to chat."

"Not quite."

"You can't quit," he reminded her. "You signed the contact."

"I know that. What I don't know is what you expect me to do! If you intended to annoy and humiliate your son, I think you succeeded. Beyond that, I'm at a loss."

"He was annoyed? Good. Humiliated? It serves him right. He has done plenty to humiliate me. And I want exactly what I said that I wanted. He is a problem. I want him not to be."

"He's thirty-two years old!"

"And he needs to grow up. He is lazy. He will not work in the company. He would prefer to be sailing his boat. Dancing attendance on unsuitable women. Creating gossip. Irritating *me*." He fixed her with a charming, conspiratorial smile. "I want it to stop."

His smile was, in its way, as handsome as his son's. But Mari felt no sizzle, only annoyance. "He won't co-operate, Mr. Costanides."

He lifted a brow. "And always your charges cooperate, Miss Lewis?" His tone was deceptively mild.

"Not always," she admitted.

"So you have ways...yes?" He looked hopeful. He made it sound like she tortured them into behaving properly.

"I teach by love and care and example," she said with an edge to her voice.

He nodded. "Just so." He steepled his hands on his desk and regarded her complacently over the top of them. "I should like to you love and care for Nikos."

A frisson of primal fear skittered down her spine. Perhaps it was because he'd used the words *love* and *Nikos* in such close proximity—even though Mari knew he didn't mean *that* kind of love!

She paced to the far end of his office and turned, with her hands on her hips. "And you think that will work?" she demanded finally, when he just looked at her expectantly.

"My dear Miss Lewis, you yourself *assured* me it would work."

"But—"

But there was nothing to say to that because, in fact, she had. And it *had* worked—with all her other charges. But this was different!

"He's not a child!" she argued.

"No, he is not. But I lost him when he was a child. I think I have to start there to get him back."

It was the first real honest remark she thought he'd made. Mari took a seat in the chair she'd been avoiding. "Why, Mr. Costanides?" She leaned her elbows on her knees and rested her chin in her palm so she could look at him as she asked quietly, "Why now?"

For a moment Stavros Costanides stared off out the window toward the beach and the ocean beyond. It was a beautiful view, but Mari didn't think he was seeing it. What *was* he seeing? Nikos? As a child? And himself? A young father? His expression grew almost pained for a moment. Then he seemed to recollect himself. His jaw tightened and he looked back at her as he admitted almost grudgingly, "I need him now."

"You didn't before?" she pressed.

He gave an irritable wave of his hand. "We don't talk about 'before.' Before is over. It is now that matters. Now and the future."

Mari didn't believe that. He'd said himself that what was happening now was a result of what had gone before. But obviously he wasn't willing to talk about it.

Stavros picked up a silver pen and tapped it on the desk, watching the movement it made for a long moment before he continued his explanation. "I want to slow down. I work too hard. Too many years too hard. I am getting old. Sixty, you know? I don't have so many years left. Two years ago I had a heart attack. Not bad, you understand. But it scares me a little. I will not live forever. I want to spend time with my wife. My children." He raised his gaze to meet hers. "You understand?"

"Children?" Mari said archly.

Stavros's mouth pressed into a thin line for a second, as he absorbed the hit, then he nodded to acknowledge it. "My *little* children. They need a father."

"And Nikos doesn't?"

"Nikos is an adult, for all that he acts like an irresponsible idiot!"

And I wonder why that is? Mari said silently. But she just waited for Stavros to continue.

"I keep my company, though," he said. "I built it!" These last three words were spoken with the most emotion she'd heard from him. "From nothing I built it. Almost thirty-five years I have invested in it. It is my life, my legacy! I won't see it wasted." His eyes met hers again, dark and fierce. "I don't let Nikos waste it!"

"You think he would?" Mari didn't know anything about that possibility.

Stavros made a spitting sound. "Bah. Why wouldn't

he?'' He picked up a folder from his desk and shoved it at her. ''See for yourself!''

Mari took the folder automatically. It was at least an inch thick, filled, she could see, with copies of newspaper clippings. Headlines like *''Greek Playboy Turns Heiress's Head''* and *''Nick the Hunk Bares All''* blared out at her. She shut the folder with a snap.

''You see? He knows nothing! He cares nothing! He respects nothing!'' Stavros's dark complexion was a deep shade of red. He aimed the pen at her. ''That is what I want you to fix.''

Helping children become emotionally healthy was something she was pretty good at. Keeping an adult man from running amok in the scandal sheets and driving a family business into the ground was not exactly in the same league.

''I'm not sure...'' she began hesitantly.

''*I* am sure.'' The pen leveled on her again. ''You will teach him to respect.''

It was on the tip of Mari's tongue to tell him that respect was earned, not taught, but she didn't think he wanted to hear it.

Stavros tapped the pen irritably on the desktop. ''He is smart. He is clever. He could do well if he wanted to. But he has to understand the business, the work I do. He won't. He behaves like a fool. Then he wants to take over just like that.'' He snapped his fingers. '''I can do it,' he says. 'Trust me,' he says. 'You want me to take over? Step down, I will take over,' he says. *Never! I* never started at the top!''

Fire blazed in Stavros's eyes. And then, as it ebbed, he got once more that faraway look, and Mari imagined that he was remembering that time thirty-five or so years ago when Costanides International had been no more than a dream. For a long moment neither of them spoke.

Then Stavros seemed to collect himself and he went on firmly, "Even so, I don't want to cut him out. He is my son. But," he added with heavy emphasis, "he is no longer my only son. I have another. Maybe I will have two others. If Nikos wants to take over, to be part of Costanides International, he must learn!"

To do it my way, Mari finished for him silently.

"I can't teach him anything about your business, Mr. Costanides."

"*I* teach him that," he said emphatically. "You teach him how to listen, to do what I say!"

"To respect," Mari said quietly, inevitably.

Stavros poked the pen-point into the blotter on his desk. "Exactly. Yes." He gave a nod of dismissal. "Go now."

Just like his son, he had a way of ending things. Mari got to her feet and started for the door.

"Miss Lewis?"

She turned back.

He pointed at her again with the silver pen, fixing her where she stood. "And you start with no more kisses. Understood?"

Nikos rolled over on his bed and pushed back the curtain, watching Mari Lewis return from the main house and wondering how in heaven's name he'd ever mistaken her for one of Debbie's Dollies. He must have overdosed on his pain medication.

With her pinned up hair and her white blouse and navy blue skirt, she really did look like some damn librarian—or a convent schoolgirl.

Still, for all that she resembled a refugee from *The*

Sound of Music, she sure didn't *kiss* like a convent schoolgirl!

Or, if she did, he'd better start taking another look at convents.

He waited, watched her...and wondered if she'd let him have another soon.

From the look on her face, he didn't think it likely. And yet—

She'd wanted it. He would swear she'd wanted it. He would swear she'd wanted *him*!

Who was the real Mari Lewis under that schoolgirl disguise? Whoever she was, she was wasted on little kids!

He hadn't been lying about his headache. It was better now, but he wasn't getting up and going to look for her. If she wanted to talk to him, she could come in here. He folded his arms under his head and waited.

He didn't have to wait long. In a moment there was a tap on the door.

"Come to share my bed?" he asked her.

"Not now," she said.

He blinked and shoved himself up against the headboard. *Not now?*

When? he wanted to ask her.

But she didn't even seem to be thinking about that. She came just inside the door and said, "There's not much love lost between you, is there?"

"Not much," Nikos agreed. "Did he spell it all out for you? His demands and my bad behavior?"

She hesitated. "He...dropped some hints."

"I'll fill you in, if you'd like."

She rubbed her forehead. "No, thanks."

"I could save us both some headaches if you'd just drive me to the airport."

"I can't do that."

"Why not?"

"I don't think that's in the plan."

"Screw his plans," Nikos said sharply. "If I didn't have this damn cast I'd be out of here so fast his head would spin."

"And give up your inheritance?"

He frowned. "What the hell do you mean by that?" *Now what was the old man up to?*

"That's what he's threatening. You don't play ball his way, do what he wants, and the company goes to Alex and the new baby."

"Let it, then!" Nikos exploded.

"He doesn't want it to. He'd rather you take over."

"But he won't let me."

"He will if—"

"I do it *his* way. No thanks."

"According to him, you need to understand how the business works."

"I *know* how businesses work!"

Mari's brows went straight up beneath the fringe of hair across her forehead. Nikos said something rude under his breath. If he shocked Miss Goody Two Shoes, he didn't care.

"I gather you don't agree you need to know."

"I don't agree I need to know."

"Then prove it," she suggested mildly, "by listening to him and showing him."

"Why the hell doesn't *he* listen to *me*?"

"I don't know," she said calmly. "I'll ask him sometime."

Nikos muttered again. "Don't bother!" He gave a dismissive wave of his hand, but she didn't move. She stood with her back to the door as if she was terrified of him, and yet oddly he didn't think she was.

"What are you waiting for?" he demanded gruffly. "Another invitation?" He patted the sheet next to him and was pleased to see the color on her face deepen.

"I'll be in the kitchen if you want me," she said, and fled, pulling the door shut behind her.

"I won't want you, sweetheart," Nikos said, but his harsh voice was only loud enough for his own ears. "Unless it's in my bed."

A vision of Mari Lewis's slender curves and ample bosom naked and delectable floated through his mind. Out of her proper clothes and with her long hair unbound, she would be something! Better than what-was-her-name—*Truffles!*—oh, God, yes.

Was he crazy? He was fantasizing about a *nanny!*

His nanny! It was almost kinky.

It had obviously been too damn long since he'd had a woman in his arms.

Mari had made a career of coping with children in trauma. She was used to coming into their lives at moments of crisis—when a parent died or a marriage shattered or a long string of broken promises left them without trust or hope.

Better than all the king's horses and all the king's men, Mari Lewis was a master at putting them together again. She gave them hope, taught them to trust themselves first and then to judge others. It was hard work. It was more than hard work—it was exhausting work at times.

But it was ever so rewarding to know she'd made a difference.

She'd believed she could make just such a difference to Nikos Costanides—when she'd believed he was four!

And now?

Well, he certainly wasn't four, and the trauma, whatever it was, went a lot deeper. But that didn't make him any less needy. She could almost see the need crying out from deep inside him.

Oh, yes. That's definitely what you're interested in, she jeered at herself.

Well, okay. She wasn't only interested in his pain and his miserable childhood. She was also interested in Nikos as a man.

But the man was a product of his upbringing, wasn't he? And it was her job to deal with that.

She knew without giving it a thought what his reaction would be. *Forget it.* She was sure he'd said it plenty of times. *I don't need that son-of-a-bitch!* She could almost hear him say those words, too.

But why?

What had happened between Nikos and his father to bring them to this?

The folder Stavros had given her sat on the desk in her bedroom. She had put it there the moment she'd returned. She hadn't picked it up. She didn't want to pick it up.

She wanted to get to know Nikos for herself.

And then what?

Put the family back together again. Of course.

And?

And nothing, she told herself sharply. She was doing her job, that was all.

And what about the kiss? What about the sizzle?

Did Mary Poppins ever have to think about things like that?

CHAPTER THREE

THE phone rang at three a.m.

Mari, startled out of a restless sleep, wasn't even sure where she was for a moment. When she finally remembered, it wasn't an improvement. Was Stavros Costanides doing a bed-check? she wondered.

She groped for the phone on her bedside table. But when she picked it up, she discovered that Nikos was already on the line.

And so was a soft-voiced woman with a British accent. "Ah, Nikos," she said, "I got you up."

"Again," Mari heard Nikos growl sleepily. "You never let me get a full night's sleep, Claudia."

The woman on the other end of the line giggled.

Hastily Mari slammed the phone down. She shouldn't have been surprised. She *wasn't* surprised. Annoyed was more like it.

Annoyed because she'd been awakened. Not because Nikos Costanides had another woman! Mari rolled over and punched her pillow, then settled her head down again. She didn't care. She had no reason to care.

Only the memory of his kiss. And that incredible sizzle.

She hard-boiled his egg. She burned his toast. She had to start over with both before she got them the way she always fixed them. And then she carried them on a tray to his bedroom and tapped on the door.

If he'd been four, she'd have walked in.

51

She wasn't walking in on *this* Nikos Costanides.

"Come in," he growled.

She pushed the door open and pasted a bright good-morning smile on her face. A good thing, too, because if she'd waited to try to do it until she'd actually confronted him, ruffled and sleepy, sprawled in his bed with the sheet barely pulled over the most private parts of him, she doubted if she could have made her muscles work.

As it was, she managed to swallow and that was about it.

"Come to cuddle?" he drawled, and gave her what was undoubtedly one of his better playboy leers.

She remembered Thomas saying he liked to tease, and knew that she was the butt of this particular joke. She wondered what he would do if she said yes!

Not that she was going to! she reminded herself smartly. Curiosity killed the cat, after all. Who was to say she was immune?

It was enough to know that whatever spark had existed between her and Nikos Costanides, it had lasted to live another day.

"I've brought you some breakfast," she said, crossing the room and setting the tray on the table.

He stared at it. "Boiled egg and toast fingers?" He sounded incredulous.

"I can fix oatmeal if you'd like."

"Being a nanny entails fixing breakfast?"

"Generally, yes. Especially since we're, um…on our own down here." She wasn't sure she wanted to call attention to that, but since it was obvious, she didn't suppose it made any difference. He wasn't dim.

"I see. And then what do you do? Teach me my numbers? Help my tie my shoes?"

"I do whatever needs to be done," Mari said. "Manners, in this case, I should think."

A grin slashed across his dark features. "Ouch." But he shoved himself up further to get in position to take the tray. The duvet covering him slipped another inch or so, and Mari's eyes shifted in that direction. The look Nikos gave her was silently amused.

She prayed he wouldn't comment, though. It was one thing to acknowledge "sizzle." It was another to want to rip the covers off him and study his naked form!

Just how she knew he was naked under that duvet, she didn't want to think. She couldn't recall *ever* thinking about Ward's state of dress or undress, even when she'd brought him breakfast in bed during his occasional weekend visits to The Folly, her aunts' old Victorian house.

"No coffee?" Nikos asked hopefully as she set the tray on his lap. "Or am I getting cocoa instead?"

"I...I'll get you some coffee," Mari said quickly. "Anything else?"

He raised one dark brow. "You?"

She fled.

With her hair pulled back into a ponytail and no makeup on her face, Mari Lewis still looked like a bit player in *Sister Act* when she carried that boiled egg and those ridiculous toast fingers into his room. At least she was dressed more informally in a pair of slacks and a scoopneck rose-colored T-shirt.

To match her rose-colored glasses, Nikos thought as he picked up his fork and poked at the egg. He hadn't had a boiled egg in years. His mother was the last person to ever make him a boiled egg, and he thought he must have been about ten at the time.

He felt about ten right now. Stubborn and cranky and up to no good.

He stabbed the egg. His stomach growled. *Damn it*. He gritted his teeth, feeling betrayed by his body as well as by everything else. He set down his fork. Glared at the egg. Glared at the toast. Glared at the door through which Mari Lewis had departed.

His stomach growled again. Reluctantly, irritably, he picked up his fork and took a bite.

The egg was good. The toast was crisp and golden, lightly buttered. Perfection. *Hell!* He ate them both in moments.

His only solace was that Mari Lewis appeared equally astonished at the empty tray when she came back with the coffee.

"Would you like another?" she asked. "I didn't give you very much. I'm used to cooking for smaller appetites."

He was tempted to say something smart, but she hadn't spoken mockingly, so he didn't either. Actually, the egg and toast had hit the spot. His father's cook, Alana, who had sent down meals, did an excellent job, but she tended to make exotic things that very pregnant women had cravings for and their very wealthy husbands felt inclined to indulge.

Nikos didn't mind the meals she sent down—it was better than having to fix his own—but there was something oddly comforting about the stupid boiled egg and toast.

It was a nice thing to eat when you felt like hell.

He felt like hell.

He hadn't slept much last night. Being thwarted never did much for his ability to get a good night's sleep. And his father's latest salvo had made him fume and toss and turn for hours. And just when he'd finally got to sleep Claudia had called.

He'd spent an hour on the phone with her. And after that he hadn't been able to sleep. Consequently, his headache, which on normal days stayed pretty controllable, was already nagging at his temples. He couldn't do much for it. But his stomach was another matter.

"I wouldn't mind another egg," he allowed now.

"Or two?" Mari Lewis asked.

He hesitated. Then, "Two," he agreed gruffly. "And some more toast," he added as she turned back toward the kitchen. "I would have expected you to do toy soldier toast men actually," he gibed.

"I do," she said, "for good little boys."

He stuck out his tongue at her.

She laughed.

Her whole face lit up when she laughed. Her blue-green eyes sparkled and the few freckles on her cheeks seemed almost to dance, and her mouth looked more kissable than ever. Nikos felt a very strong urge to do just that. And he would—the next time she got close enough.

"Two pieces of toast," he answered her. "Please."

The word came out unbidden, though it didn't surprise him really. He was generally more polite than he'd been to Mari Lewis. Not that she didn't deserve a little shortness, as agent of his father's misplaced behavior modification program!

She grinned delightedly, as if she'd won a round, and he frowned fiercely at her. It didn't stop her smiling. And he had to wait until she'd gone into the other room to close his eyes and rub his aching head.

His eyes were still closed a few minutes later when she returned.

"Here you go." A clean dish materialized in front of him with two more perfectly done boiled eggs. Beside it, with a flourish, she set a plate of toast fingers—cut like toy soldiers.

Nikos goggled at them, then at her.

Mari Lewis smiled impishly at him. "You said please," she said, before darting out of his reach.

Damn, but he wanted to kiss her!

"Is he a nice little boy, darling?" Aunt Emmaline asked.

And how am I supposed to answer that? Mari wondered. She bent her bare toes over the rung of the kitchen stool and glanced over her shoulder toward the bedroom where she'd left Nikos and his toast and eggs minutes before. *Fine as long as he stayed right where he was,* she thought. But she glanced over her shoulder every few seconds, it seemed, to make sure he did. She'd had the definite impression that if he'd been able to, he would have grabbed her when she'd brought him that toast and eggs.

And then what would he have done? she wondered. *Kissed her?*

There was that possibility. *And that's bad?*

Of course it was. There was Claudia, after all.

Whoa! Wait just a minute. You aren't angling to marry him, only to kiss him, to discover the extent of your own passion. Well, in that case...

But even so, she thought she needed a little more time, a little more space, a little more preparation. She didn't want to be caught off-guard the way she had been the first time.

"Mari? Are you there? Do we have a bad connection? I asked you about Nikos."

"He's, um...fine," she fumbled. "Most of the time."

"Not as badly behaved as you'd feared?"

"Different than I'd feared." That was certainly the truth!

"But you can handle him," Aunt Em said with her perennial confidence. "Did you say his father was a widower?"

Aunt Em was always on the lookout for Ward's replacement. She'd never thought he was good enough for her niece. After Shelley, Mari had no trouble agreeing with her.

"His father is remarried," she explained. "And the little boy's name is Alex."

"Alex?" This was Aunt Bett on the extension. "I thought you said his name was Nikos."

"I thought it was. I...was mistaken." But she wasn't about to make the mistake of telling her aunts anything about the true nature of her job! They fussed about her enough. One word about the real Nikos Costanides and the fussing would reach a new level altogether.

"I get Thursday off." She changed the subject. "I'll be around to see you then." Their house on Orient Point was about an hour's drive from the Costanides place.

"Will you be bringing Alex?" Aunt Em asked eagerly.

"No," Mari said. "Days off imply just that, Aunt Em. I don't have to bring him."

"Bring whom? Where?" a masculine voice said right behind her.

Mari jumped a foot. She jerked around to see Nikos leaning on his crutches and regarding her with amusement from the hallway. Damn it! How could he walk so soundlessly when he was using a cast and crutches, for heaven's sake?

She put her hand over the receiver. "This is a private conversation!"

"It's a pack of lies," he said genially. "Who're you talking to?"

"It is not!" Mari defended herself.

"Is that the little boy's father?" Aunt Em asked. "What a nice strong voice he has."

Mari removed her hand, since it wasn't doing any good anyway. "Isn't it?" Mari said. Then to Nikos, she hissed, "None of your business. Go away."

"If I'm your business, you're mine, sweetheart. Give me the phone. I'll tell the truth."

"No!" She had no intention of giving him the phone and letting him talk to her aunts! She should have waited to call them. But she'd promised them that she would call once she got settled in. They had known she wouldn't call the first night, but they did worry, so she wanted to let them know all was well—even if it wasn't!

Nikos cocked his head and grinned coaxingly. "Please?" He said the word mockingly, and she wished she'd never given him those damned toy soldier toast fingers!

"I have to go now," she said quickly to her aunts. "He's misbehaving."

"Begin as you mean to go on," Aunt Em advised.

"Spare the rod, spoil the child," Aunt Bett intoned.

"Oh, yes," Mari agreed. "I'll call you later." She hung up and stood to face him. He wasn't more than four inches taller than she was, yet he seemed so much bigger. And so very…male. She ran her tongue over her lips.

Nikos didn't stop grinning. "Misbehaving, am I?"

"Badly," Mari affirmed. "My aunt thinks I should take a switch to you."

He lifted a brow. "Kinky, is she?"

Mari felt her cheeks flame. "She's a very proper eighty-one-year-old lady with strict ideas of how children should be raised."

Nikos still grinned. "I'd like to meet her."

"Not on your life! Have you finished with your breakfast?"

"Yes. But I couldn't manage the tray and the crutches."

"You don't need to bring it in. I'll come and get it. You should stay in bed."

"I'm not that much of an invalid."

"Perhaps not. But you didn't get much sleep, did you?"

He frowned. "How did you know that?"

"I heard the phone. I picked it up and—" She stopped, not wanting to admit hearing the lilting English voice of the woman who'd called him.

"Oh, Claudia." A sort of wry smile touched his face. "She thinks I've got insomnia so she never cares when she calls."

So Claudia was his girlfriend. It must be a pretty intense relationship if she felt free enough to call him at any hour of the day or night. "And Claudia is...?" she ventured, hoping that he would expand on that.

"Important," he said firmly. "Whenever she calls, you get me, understand?"

Mari blinked at the firmness of his tone. She swallowed, then nodded her head. "Of course."

"Even if I'm in the shower. *Especially* if I'm in the shower." A grin flashed across his face.

Mari felt her cheeks turning red. How dare he come on to *her* when he was talking about another woman!

The phone rang just then and she said frostily, "In

this case, I won't need to get you at all." And she brushed past him to go get the tray, leaving him to answer it.

"Costanides," Nikos growled into the receiver. There was a second's pause, then, "Go to hell," he said to whoever was on the other end, and slammed the receiver down.

"Not Claudia?" Mari asked over her shoulder.

"Your esteemed employer," he said through his teeth. The phone rang again.

Nikos ignored it. It rang again. And again. "I'm not answering it." He fitted his crutches beneath his arms and hobbled away from the phone. "He's your boss, not mine."

Mari stared at him, then at the phone. She didn't much want to answer it, either. She didn't want to hear any more lectures from Stavros on respect. And she didn't need him looking over her shoulder every second. She didn't particularly want to answer the phone in front of Nikos, either. But she knew Stavros well enough to know that he'd keep right on ringing until someone answered it.

She stalked over and snatched it up. "Yes?"

"Ah, Miss Lewis," Stavros's unmistakable Greek-accented English rasped in her ear. "And how are things today?"

Mari's teeth came together. "They *were* fine."

She saw Nikos stiffen and stop at her tone. He turned to look at her.

"He is behaving badly already?" Stavros's voice became angry. "I did not think—! He has always been good to women! Despite everything else, he has shown *them* respect! But to you he is—!"

"He's fine, Mr. Costanides," Mari cut in. "But I can't

focus on him if you're calling me all the time. I need time with him. Alone. Without your interference.''

There was stunned silence on the other end of the line. Nikos broke into a grin. Mari glared at him.

''Respect is—''

''Respect is something that takes time to develop, Mr. Costanides,'' she said as evenly as she could. ''Especially when you've wasted opportunities to develop it over the years.''

''I—''

''I appreciate your concern. But please, let me do my job.''

''Yes, yes. Your job. You— ''

''I need you to give us space. Time.''

''Privacy,'' Nikos murmured with a wicked grin on his face.

Mari turned her back on him. ''You reward his worst behaviour, Mr. Costanides. If you constantly check up on us and fuss about every little thing...''

''Fuss? *I?* Fuss?'' Stavros sounded outraged.

''Get upset,'' Mari corrected herself. Clearly the self-concept of a sixty-year-old Greek patriarch did not include ''fussing.'' ''I appreciate your concern, Mr. Costanides, but I really must handle Nikos on my own.''

Over her shoulder, she could hear the soft sound of Nikos applauding. She stiffened her back, and her resolve not to turn around and look at him.

''I only try to help,'' Stavros said, wounded.

''Then give me the space I need. And silent support.''

''Silent?''

''Silent,'' Mari repeated firmly.

She got silence. She wasn't sure about the support. But finally, about the time she thought she was listening to dead air, Stavros said worriedly, ''He is treating you all right?''

''He is treating me fine.'' That was, if she ignored his more flagrantly teasing remarks, he was treating her fine.

''You're sure?''

''I'm positive, Mr. Costanides.'' She wanted to hang up. She wanted to say, *Oh, for heaven's sake, leave me alone.*

She didn't, because she knew if she did, he would be over here in five minutes, sticking his nose in, making things fifty times worse. She had no idea if she could do what he wanted or not. But she knew quite well *he* couldn't do it with his methods. If he had been able to, he'd have managed it years ago.

''You will call if you need me?''

''Certainly.''

''You don't take disrespect?''

''Of course not.''

He made a harumphing sound, one that said he wasn't *quite* convinced, but... ''Very well, Miss Lewis. I give you space.''

''Thank you, Mr. Costanides.'' She started to hang up.

''We will see you at lunchtime.''

''We won't be here at lunchtime.''

''Not here? But—''

''Nikos and I need time together. Alone,'' Mari said as quietly as she could, all the while moving as far away from the man standing in the hall behind her as she could.

Obviously, from the gleeful, ''Hear, hear,'' coming from Nikos, she hadn't moved far enough. She turned and glared.

Nikos grinned unrepentantly.

"I have to go, Mr. Costanides. There are matters here that need my attention."

"Nikos? Is he—?"

"Goodbye, Mr. Costanides. I'll call you in a few days."

"Days?" she heard him begin to sputter, but she didn't stop to listen to anymore. She hung up. She faced Nikos and dared him to tease her now.

He regarded her solemnly. The grin he'd been wearing had vanished when she put the receiver down, and his brows hiked up beneath the fringe of disheveled dark hair that straggled across his forehead.

"Whoa," he said, and he sounded not sarcastic or teasing, but almost respectful. "Guess you told him."

"I said what had to be said."

"And what no one else has ever dared say before," Nikos said drily.

"You appear to have told him a few less than palatable things over the years," Mari pointed out. "I can't believe I'm the first person to thwart him."

"Maybe not. But you might be the first one he's listened to."

"We don't know that he's listened yet, do we?" Mari said, a little apprehensive that Stavros might at this very moment be striding across the grass that separated the big house from Nikos's small cottage.

As if he'd read her mind, Nikos crutched his way over to the window and tipped the blind aside so he could look up at his father's house. "Nobody coming," he said. "And no cannons being aimed in our direction."

Mari managed a smile. "That's good news, I suppose." She felt a little weak in the knees now that the conversation was over.

"So, where are we going?" Nikos asked.

"What?"

"You told him we weren't going to be here at lunch-time," he reminded her. "I wondered where we were going to be."

"Oh. Right." She smiled a little guiltily. "I don't know. I just knew that putting the two of you together right now wasn't going to accomplish anything."

"It would make him mad." Nikos didn't look as if that would dismay him at all.

"Which is not what I want to do, even if you do," Mari said sharply. "But I suppose you're right. We should go somewhere. Would you like to go for a drive?"

Nikos smiled and shifted on his crutches, stretching slightly. It ought to have looked as if he was adjusting something that annoyed him, instead it seemed to her a decidedly sexy stretch. He was still bare-chested, which gave her quite a lot of uncovered masculine flesh to study. But when he stretched his shorts dropped another inch and she got even more!

"I'd like that very much." And it sounded less as if he'd said the words and more as if he'd actually *purred* them!

She'd stuck up for him!

He couldn't believe it. In his entire life, only one person had ever stuck up for Nikos with his father—his mother.

Like a lioness protecting her cub, Angelika Costanides had fought with her husband again and again—rejecting his father's seemingly endless demands that he change schools, move to Greece, study at a particular university, take certain courses, work in the family business, marry the right woman.

"He is not you!" Angelika said over and over. "Let him alone!"

"He needs to know! To learn!" Stavros countered.

And his mother always replied heavily, "He'll know. He'll learn all he needs to soon enough."

By that time in the conversation, there was always such a wealth of pain in her voice that Nikos wanted to slam in and break it up, to throw his father out, to comfort his mother's anguish.

Always he waited, impotently and furiously, until his father nodded his head and said in a cold remote voice, "Just as you wish, Angelika," and disappeared out of their lives once again.

And then she would turn to Nikos, pacing and fuming in his wake, and say, "He is your father. You must respect that."

"I don't respect *him*," he told his mother every time.

"Ah, Nikos." She put her hand on his arm and he allowed her to drag him into a gentle embrace. At first he had been small enough to press his face into her breasts. But at the last he could rest his chin on the top of her head. He would feel her shake her head gently and say words he never understood. "Poor Stavros. He can't help it. He tries."

As far as Nikos could see, the old man didn't try at all. Except to cause hurt and pain to his wife—a woman who had given him everything she had in terms of both worldly wealth and womanly devotion for her whole life.

It had been an arranged marriage, Nikos knew that. He supposed that was why his father didn't care. Stavros had married her, Nikos was sure, for the money that her family had. He'd never really cared about the woman who'd come with it. They hadn't lived together since Nikos was eight years old.

And yet he knew, despite their separation, that his mother had always loved her husband. She would never let Nikos speak badly of him. She never said a bad thing herself. She just looked sad. And lonely. And she'd been alone—except for her son—when she'd died of a heart attack six years ago.

The death of his mother was the most painful loss Nikos had ever experienced. He'd been grief-stricken, missing her terribly, devastated by her loss, even though intellectually he should have been prepared.

For over a year he'd known she had a bad heart. She hadn't wanted to tell him, but eventually she couldn't hide it anymore. She was too pale, too weak to pretend. For some time after he'd settled in Britain, he didn't see her as often as he would have liked. She hadn't minded.

"You have your life," she'd said. "You must do what you must do."

She'd never made the demands his father had. It had been a shock, then, to come flying in for a visit and find her much paler than he remembered her. During their visit, she'd tired easily, too. He'd asked what was wrong; she'd dismissed it. He'd let her get away with it then. Perhaps, he thought, it was only the result of the bronchitis she'd had in the winter. But he came back a month later and she'd been no better. She was worse.

That was when she'd had to tell him. He had believed it. He'd done everything he could to get her to find a cardiologist who could help her.

"I've done all I can," she assured him. "There is nothing left."

Nothing but coming back as often as he could. He flew in nearly every weekend that last year. He spent the last month of her life with her.

He'd never seen Stavros there.

So his father's claim to grief—the old man had wept beside her grave, for heaven's sake—had seemed like just so much false emotion to Nikos.

"Where were you when she was alive?" he'd demanded harshly before they even left the cemetery.

And if his father had still looked ashen, Nikos didn't care. The old man was a good actor! He couldn't fool the young man who'd been by his mother's side for twenty-six years when his father had been everywhere else but home.

And as far as Nikos was concerned, Stavros had proved it a year later when he'd married Julietta, a woman young enough to be his daughter!

All Nikos could say about that was that his old man had good taste. Hell, yes, Julietta was lovely! So lovely that Nikos himself had actually dated her a few times.

But she'd been too prim and proper and too "old line Greek" for him. She was controlled by her family much the same way his mother had been controlled.

He supposed she had her family to thank for her ridiculous marriage to his father, too!

Though, he had to admit, you wouldn't know it to look at them. What a devoted little family they'd become—Stavros, Julietta, and their own little Alexander. Smiling, happy. Hugging and talking and laughing together. A perfect little threesome. And now they had a new baby on the way.

Nikos gritted his teeth whenever he stopped to think about his father's new happy little brood.

He knew he shouldn't begrudge Stavros the joy of his second marriage—however insane it might be. And when he was feeling sane and sober and sensible, Nikos wished them all well.

He even occasionally found himself hoping that the

old man did for Alexander what he'd never done for his older son. Because it would be good for Alexander to know his father cared about him—*not* because it would be good for the old man.

He didn't give a rat's ass about his old man—or his company.

And he wasn't about to shape up because a pretty little nanny told him to!

She was a pretty little nanny, though, Nikos thought. And she *had* taken his part this morning. Not to mention the way she kissed.

Going for a drive with her might be the best thing that had happened to him in a long while!

Going out for a drive with him was not the brightest idea she'd ever had. The confines of a car were bound to make her even more aware of him. As if she weren't aware enough already!

But she didn't see that she had any choice. If she wanted to make an effort to do her job—to help foster a real reconciliation between Nikos and his father—she was going to have to keep Stavros at arm's length.

That she could—and would—do.

The trouble was going to be keeping Nikos at arm's length as well.

It was interesting how *aware* she was of him. Her reactions were nothing like the ones she'd had to Ward and every other man she'd ever dated—not that she'd dated a vast number, of course.

Maybe she'd only dated duds.

Nikos wasn't a dud. The trouble was, he was likely to be far more man than she could handle.

"Just say no, darling," she remembered Aunt Em advising her on the subject of boys and temptation.

Up until now that had been no problem. But up until yesterday she'd never kissed Nikos.

It was like playing with fire. Attractive. Tempting. Fun. Dangerous.

Children shouldn't do it. But Mari was an adult. She needed to know how to deal with fire—how to test it, fan it, encourage it, control it.

With Nikos Costanides?

She was out of her blinking mind!

She was waiting by the pool with Julietta and Alex when he finished showering, got dressed and was ready to go. He had made an effort and put on a pair of bleached canvas trousers and a dark red T-shirt in honor of the occasion. It was the first time since he'd come from the hospital that he'd bothered to put on more than a pair of ragged cut-offs or faded shorts.

Or a towel. He remembered yesterday with a smile.

His father always looked like he'd just stepped off Savile Row—even when he was "relaxing."

"You must convey a responsible image," he had said more times than Nikos wanted to count.

A "responsible image" was the last thing Nikos wanted to convey—especially when the old man was around. He had made a habit of dressing down for years. But today, for the lovely nanny, who kissed like a dream and had stuck up for him, he made a small effort. After all it was his father he was annoyed at, not her.

Whether Mari appreciated his sartorial elegance was not immediately apparent. She was talking to Julietta. He stopped, realizing that he'd have to weather Julietta's knowing smiles and inane remarks if he made his way up there. She would undoubtedly think his father saddling him with a nanny was just "too funny for words."

To someone else it probably was. Nikos set his teeth, prepared to endure the encounter. After all, he'd endured far worse.

But he didn't need to, for as soon as Mari saw him coming, she said goodbye to Julietta and hurried toward him.

Another point for the nanny. Nikos leaned on his crutches and waited for her, breathing a sigh of relief.

"Sorry," she said a little breathlessly. "I didn't mean to keep you waiting. I just wanted to see how Julietta was feeling." She had dressed for the occasion, too, in a pair of chambray slacks and a scoop-necked bright turquoise shirt. It wasn't quite the librarian garb she'd had on yesterday, but it was hardly a sexy outfit. So why was he so damned aware of her?

Because she looked as eager and well-scrubbed as a schoolgirl? Because he made it a habit to toy with innocents? Because he wanted a ride up the coast and nothing more.

No, no, and no again.

He studied her hair, which she had clamped in a barrette at the nape of her neck. It was as anchored down as she was—and yet it loosened a little and blew in the wind. Would *she* loosen? Would she let her hair down for him?

She didn't look like it. But God, had she ever kissed like it.

Remembering, trying to figure it out, Nikos limped toward the garage on his crutches and Mari walked alongside him.

"What's wrong?" she asked at his frown of concentration.

"Why don't you wear it down?"

She blinked at him. "What?"

"Your hair. It hates being confined like that."

She smiled. "You can tell, can you?"

"Yes. Absolutely. Here." He reached out a hand and deftly loosed it from the barrette she wore.

"Nikos!" She reached back and grabbed it out of his hand.

He let her have the barrette, much more interested in running a hand over her hair. It glinted in the sunlight, the deep honey color shot through with gold. It was as soft and heavy as he'd imagined it would be. He smiled.

She caught his hand and pulled it away from her hair. "No," she said.

"No?" He tried turning her hand in his, but she held on.

"No," she repeated. "You can't do that."

"I just did," he reminded her.

"But I didn't want you to."

His gaze narrowed. "You did, too."

A hint of red touched her cheeks. She shook her head. "I didn't."

He just looked at her.

Her gaze slid away. "I shouldn't," she qualified gruffly after a moment.

A corner of Nikos's mouth quirked at her honesty. "A nanny never lies?"

Her color deepened. "I try not to." She refused to look at him, keeping her eyes cast down. She reminded him for all the world of Maria, the misbehaving postulant in *The Sound of Music* that his mother had taken him to see when he was a child.

He wanted to argue with her. He wanted to tell her he was teasing, that it was no more than play between men and women, and that it would lead them exactly where they wanted to go.

It wasn't like he was grabbing her and throwing her down on the grass and having his way with her, for heaven's sake! It wasn't as if he'd taken her in broad daylight and kissed her senseless! It wasn't—

He stopped. He remembered.

He remembered yesterday. Julietta and all her friends had been up by the pool and Nikos had come out the door, wearing only a towel. And he'd taken Mari into his arms and kissed her. Deeply. Hungrily. Possessively.

Senselessly.

He shut his eyes. When he opened them again, she was still standing there, eyes downcast, unmoving.

He sighed. "Turn around."

She flicked a quick glance up at him. "What?"

He took hold of her shoulder gently and turned her. "Turn around."

She must have realized what he was doing then, for she turned. She stood with her back to him. And Nikos, leaning heavily against his crutches, took hold of that golden honeyed shank of hair and pulled it back into his hand. Then, because he couldn't quite behave perfectly, he combed his fingers through it for just a moment. Finally, though, reluctantly, but firmly, he fastened the barrette into place once more.

"There." He let his hands drop.

Mari turned back to face him and the smile she gave him was almost worth it. "Thank you, Nikos." She looked like Maria-the-nun again.

He shut his eyes. *Ah, Mari Lewis, what am I going to do with you?*

CHAPTER FOUR

MARI didn't know what she would have done if he hadn't given her back the barrette.

It was one thing to draw the line with a four-year-old. It was something else entirely to have to put down limits with a man the tabloids called Nick the Hunk. There was no real way she could count on them being honored—except by an appeal to respect.

And she feared it was much too early for that. Besides, according to Stavros, Nikos knew nothing about respect.

So why had he given her back the barrette?

Of course he'd taken his own sweet time about it, turning her and touching her and combing his fingers through her hair and sending a whole raftload of sizzles through her. But he'd done what she asked.

She had sizzle—and she had control. She gave a small skip of sheer satisfaction.

She could do this. She *could!*

Nikos pressed a remote garage door opener as they approached the building, and by the time they arrived, the door had rolled up to reveal four gleaming cars.

"Take your pick," he said, "since you're going to be driving."

Mari looked them over and swallowed hard. Like Nikos, they were all out of her league. Big and shiny and dangerous or small and sleek and lethal. And every one worth far more than she would make in a year.

"How about taking mine? I know how to drive it."

73

Nikos grinned. "The principles are the same no matter what the car."

"I don't think—"

"You want me to be brave and grow up willing to try new things, don't you?" Nikos asked, his dark eyes glinting with wicked humor and challenge.

Mari groaned. "That is tripe."

Nikos laughed delightedly. "I bet you don't say that to all your charges."

She shook her head, sighing, but still smiling. "Just the ones old enough to understand."

"Right. Then, how about this?" The smile on his face vanished. "I respect your ability to do it." The humor had faded from his eyes, but the challenge didn't. He regarded her intently.

It was called being hoist by your own petard, and she knew it. "Damn," she murmured.

Nikos made a disapproving sound.

Mari swallowed a smile. "Drat," she amended sulkily. Then, in the face of his grin, she sucked in her breath and nodded. She would try it. She could call it another exercise in control.

Nikos beamed. "So, what's your choice? New and stuffy? New and stodgy? New and fast or—" and here he drew her around to see a low, sleek hunter green Jaguar convertible "—or old and fast and classy as hell."

It was clear which one he wanted her to pick.

Mari had never driven a car like the Jaguar in her life. She had a seven-year-old compact car with a dented front right fender. Her aunts favored large American sedans of a certain vintage that resembled a cross between gun boats and land barges to Mari.

"Safety first," Aunt Em always said.

This car was anything but. Mari gave a last longing thought toward her small serviceable car, her staid predictable cold fish life, and drew a deep breath.

"Old and fast and classy as hell," she said.

She didn't drive like Maria-the-nun.

Oh, granted, she'd taken it slow at first, moving up the drive with the speed of a sailboat caught in a calm. But then she'd got through town and hit the open road and, slowly but surely, her foot went down on the accelerator and the car speeded up. In a matter of minutes, it was like the wind had risen, and far from being becalmed now they were moving swiftly.

Nikos felt as if he'd been let out of prison.

His eyes opened wider. His heart beat more easily. For the first time since the accident, he could breathe.

Since he'd been confined at the cottage, he hadn't made any effort to hobble up to the pool or over to the beach. Any ventures out ran the risk of another confrontation with Stavros. His head already ached enough without that. So he'd stayed in. He had enough to keep him busy, though his father would never believe it. He'd even assured himself it was all right, that he would be fine until he got the damned cast off and finished the medication. He hadn't realized until now just how badly he'd needed to get out.

At midweek the traffic was less than on the weekends, and as they drove further out on the coast toward Montauk, it got even thinner. He breathed deeper, then glanced over to see how Mari was doing.

She was smiling, her earlier white-knuckled grip relaxed.

"How you doing?"

She laughed. "I feel like I've got a hundred wild horses at the end of a very thin rein."

"More like two hundred and sixty-five."

"Yikes." She shot him a horrified look.

"You'll feel better if you're part of the elements," he told her. "Pull over."

"What?"

"Stop on the shoulder up there." He directed her to the gravel alongside the roadway. When she stopped, Nikos moved to get out. It wasn't easy. He cursed his inability to negotiate cramped spaces with his cast and ribs, but finally he got out of the car, then started to put the top down.

"What are you doing?" Mari yelped.

"Putting you in the elements," Nikos said.

"I don't—"

"You'll love it," he said firmly, and gave her an encouraging grin.

She got out and put her hands on her hips. "If I argue, you'll tell me I should be setting an example for you so that you're willing to try new experiences."

His grin widened. "You're catching on. Here. Help me with this."

If she hadn't, he didn't know if he'd have been able to manage by himself. But after a moment's hesitation, she did, and within moments they had the top down.

"Now," he said, "you'll get the feel of things."

"Literally," Mari said drily. But she didn't look unhappy.

They got underway slowly again, but as the breeze caught her hair and lifted it, tugging it from the confines of the barrette and doing what he'd wanted to do, she flexed her fingers on the steering wheel and they didn't look so white-knuckled any longer. A few more miles per hour and she lifted her chin, letting the wind caress her face. She smiled.

"Terrible, isn't it?" he shouted at her over the wind.

"Awful." But she flashed him a brilliant smile.

He lay his arm along the back of the seat just behind her. Her honey-colored hair blew across his hand. He let his fingers tangle in it. "Amazing what those new experiences will do."

She stuck out her tongue at him.

Oh, very good. Way to go. There's a good example you're setting, Mari Lewis, she chastised herself. *Just stick your tongue out and get right down to his level.*

But she couldn't keep a stern demeanor, not even when she knew she ought to. She was enjoying this too much.

Stavros would be appalled. He would think she'd been taken over by the enemy!

It wasn't true, Mari told herself.

She was in control. She had never had so much speed and power under her command before. It was a little terrifying. And exhilarating as all get out!

And if Stavros asked, she could say she was simply trying to understand the world the way Nikos saw it. It helped to try to put herself in the shoes of the child. If she saw life the way the child saw it, she usually had a better idea of how to help them deal with.

She didn't know, of course, if the same thing applied to thirty-two-year-olds called Nick the Hunk. But she assured herself that it must.

And the Jaguar was marvelous regardless!

She was glad he'd virtually dared her to drive it. It was so different from driving any car she'd ever driven before. Like he was so different from any man she'd kissed before. She had thought she would just go to Amagansett and turn around, but when they got there, she didn't want to stop. So she kept right on, heading toward Montauk.

There she basically ran out of road, and that was when she finally slowed down. "Do you want to go back yet or would you like to stop and get something to eat?"

"Lunch sounds good." Nikos said. He was smiling, too. It was a heady experience just looking at him. Even with his fading bruises and battered face, he looked vibrant, alive—and even more dangerous than the Jaguar.

But the danger wasn't scary, even though perhaps it ought to have been. On the contrary, Mari found herself intrigued by it, enticed, eager to know it—to know *him*—better.

Purely professionally, of course.

Oh, yes. Sure. Drat, but she wished she were better at lying to herself.

Nikos directed her to a small café near the beach. It was off the beaten track and clearly wasn't frequented by tourists. But when Nikos opened the door, he got a profuse welcome.

"Hey, Nick, honey! How are you? We heard about your accident!" The waitress, a buxom woman in her fifties hurried over, gushing motherly concern. "What happened?"

"Just a little run-in with a tree," Nikos said easily.

"You sure?" The woman looked worried. "There was a picture in the paper. It looked mighty bad. You sit down here. Rollie, Nikos is here!" she hollered toward the kitchen.

A stout, fiftyish man in jeans and a white shirt poked his head out. "Hey, Nick! How ya doin'?"

Nikos shrugged. "Better. Fine now."

The man called Rollie looked him up and down. "Don't look fine." Then he eyed Mari and a speculative grin touched his mouth. "Well, some things do." He waggled his eyebrows at Nikos.

"She's a friend of my father's."

Rollie laughed. "Yeah, sure. You're just saying that 'cause you don't want Nita to be jealous."

Nita, Mari gathered, was the waitress. She was a good twenty years older than Nick, but she clearly found him as intriguing as Mari did, which should not have surprised her. Nikos Costanides was the sort of man *all* women would notice.

Would his kisses make them all sizzle? Mari wondered.

"Sit down, friend of Nikos's father," Rollie said now. "What'll you have?"

Mari glanced around. There didn't appear to be any menus, just a blackboard with the daily specials written on it. "What's good?" she asked Nikos.

"All the fish. Fresh daily."

"A codfish sandwich, then," she said. "And iced tea."

"Same for me," Nikos told the waitress. "But I'd like a beer."

"Sure thing, sweetheart," she replied. "You gonna sit in here or out there?" There was a patio with half a dozen tables alongside the café, sheltered from the off-shore breeze. Nikos looked at Mari.

"Outside, please," she said.

They went outside, and Mari took a seat at a table overlooking the beach. There were two other couples and a large family already out there, talking and laughing and eating. A couple of children were squabbling over some French fries. A golden retriever sat on the other side of the patio railing, looking hopeful as sandwiches were consumed. Nikos settled carefully into the chair opposite her, and propped his crutches against the railing.

"What a wonderful place," Mari said.

"It is," he agreed.

"There's a place a little bit like it near where my aunts live on Orient Point."

Nikos's brows went up. "Were you raised around here?"

"On the north shore."

"I was, too. Part of the time anyway," he said. "My mother lived near Greenport."

Mari knew that quite a lot of Greek-American families had homes or summer homes in that area of Long Island. She hadn't expected that Nikos's family would have, though. She'd have imagined they would go back to Greece when they weren't in New York City. "Was your mother from the U.S., then?"

He shook his head. "No. From Greece."

"Then why—?"

"Because my father was from here. And even after he never came around anymore, she wouldn't leave him. God knows why," he added harshly.

There were half a dozen landmines in those few words, and Mari knew it. She picked her way carefully. "Your parents weren't...together?"

"You mean the old man didn't tell you he ditched my mother?"

"I understood she had died."

"Six years ago. But he left her long before that."

Long before? "How old were you?"

"Eight."

Old enough to miss his father dreadfully. Her own

father had died when she was only a few years older, and it had been terrible. How much worse it would be, she thought, to lose a father and know he was still alive—just not with you.

She began to understand a bit of the estrangement between Stavros Costanides and his son.

"You stayed with your mother?"

"Yes." A muscle in his jaw ticked and he looked away, deliberately turning his attention to the golden retriever. He snapped his fingers and, when the dog came over, scratched him behind the ears. He didn't look at Mari again. "What about you?" he asked her after a moment. "How did you end up working for my old man?"

"He saw an article in a magazine," Mari said. She felt a little self-conscious bringing it up. It had been mostly hype, but there had been a core of truth to it. "It made me sound like the answer to the troubled parent's prayer."

"Are you?" Now he was looking at her. And the steadiness of his gaze was even more unnerving than the question.

"I try. Mostly I succeed."

"You think you're going to succeed with me?"

"I'm going to try," she said.

He shook his head. "Waste of time."

"You don't know."

"I *do* know, sweetheart. The old man and I have spent too many years at odds to patch things up now."

"But—"

"We have. It's hopeless. And in a week I'll have the cast off and I'll be gone."

"A week?" How on earth was she going to do anything in a week?

"A week. I have places to go, people to see. And no interest in staying here at all."

Anita the waitress appeared just then with their sandwiches. "Lola was asking about you just the other day, Nick," she told him as she set his plate down.

"How is Lola? Tell her hi." He took a bite of his sandwich. "Tell her I miss her."

"And Lucy. You know Lucy. She'd follow you to the moon."

Nikos's smile widened. "Lucy, too."

When Anita left Mari looked at him speculatively. "So many women, so little time?"

Now his grin flashed her way. "Something like that."

Mari couldn't believe the stab of annoyance she felt. Was this possessiveness? Jealousy?

Surely not.

She didn't even know the man! She certainly had no claim on him. Just because she'd kissed him, been kissed *by* him—

She tried to shove the feeling away. Tried to remind herself how inappropriate it was—how inappropriate *he* was!

Just because she'd reacted to him sexually, she had no right to be jealous of his interest in other women.

He certainly wouldn't be interested in her!

And if the memory of that folder Stavros had pressed on her, and Anita's passing references to other women didn't convince her, ten minutes later the aforementioned Lucy showed up in person.

Of course Mari didn't know it was Lucy when a woman in her very early twenties, a dark-haired vivacious beauty, shouted, "Nicky!" when she spied him on the patio and practically leaped the railing to get to him.

"Hey, Lucy! How's it going?" He didn't rise, just held out a hand to her.

She swooped down, kissing him on the mouth, then stepped back and said,

"Oh, Nicky, darling! Your poor face. And your leg! Are you all right?"

He gave the same dismissive answer to her that he had given the waitress. And Mari had to give him grudging credit for not taking advantage of all the sympathy he could have elicited from them. "No big deal. I'm fine," he assured Lucy when she continued to gush and fret.

"But—"

"Don't worry about me," he told her firmly.

"I can't help it." Lucy's lower lip went out. "You matter to me." The look she gave him was equal parts possessiveness and adoration. The one she gave Mari was meant in no uncertain terms to tell her that Nikos was taken.

"Who's she?" Lucy asked Nikos, jerking her head in Mari's direction.

"A friend," Nikos said.

Mari noticed that he didn't add *of my father's* this time. Was he using her as a buffer, then? Interesting thought.

"Mari Lewis," he said, introducing them. "Lucy Ferrante."

"Hello," Mari said genially, holding out a hand.

Lucy nodded. "Hi." Then she turned right back to Nikos. "Why didn't you call me? I'd have come to visit you."

"They wouldn't let me have visitors at the hospital."

"After then?"

"I'm staying at my father's."

"I would have come there."

Nikos didn't reply to that. He changed the subject, asked Lucy about her brothers, what each one was doing this summer, then about her parents. Lucy answered, but at every pass she tried to turn the conversation back to coming to visit Nikos.

He didn't take her up on it, but he didn't rebuff her either. He was a master when it came to dealing with women, Mari decided.

By the time Lucy left ten minutes later, prompted by the honking of a horn that belonged, she said, to her brother's Jeep, she was convinced that it was her idea not to come and see Nikos.

"It would wear you out, I know," she said, patting his arm. "You'll tell me when you're feeling well enough?"

"Of course."

"See you soon?" A hand lingered on his shoulder.

Nikos slanted a grin up at her. "Very soon," he promised.

"Nice to have met you," Mari said, though she was quite sure Lucy didn't even remember she was there.

"Oh. Yeah. You, too," Lucy said. "Take good care of yourself, Nicky." She ruffled Nikos's hair and, after another impatient beep, took off on a run.

"Nicky?"

A corner of Nikos's mouth tipped up. "We go back a long way."

"You must have changed her diapers then," Mari said tartly.

"Jealous?"

She felt her face flame and she scowled at him. "Hardly."

He grinned knowingly, but he didn't comment, and

Mari was oddly relieved when he kept his gaze on Lucy and said, "She's a good kid."

"I'm sure she wouldn't appreciate hearing you say so. She wants to 'matter.'"

He shrugged. "She does matter."

"Not the way she'd like to."

He settled back in his chair and looked at her. "Should I tell her to get lost, then?"

"I didn't mean that," Mari said quickly. "Actually," she admitted after a moment, "I think you handled it very well."

"What's this? The Mari Lewis Seal of Approval? I've finally done something right?"

"I'm sure you do a lot right," Mari said. "I'm sure you aren't all those things the papers—" She broke off, embarrassed.

"You've been doing a little research, have you?" Nikos asked. "Did you do it on your own or did the old man provide the reading material?"

Mari hesitated. "Your father gave me them," she said finally. "I haven't read them."

"Go ahead," he said gruffly. "Read your fill."

"I don't want to."

He stared at her, his dark eyes hard and angry and disbelieving. Then he shoved his chair back, got awkwardly to his feet and tossed some bills on the table. "Let's go."

Silently Mari followed him, wondering what she should have done, what she should have said.

He was standing by the car, waiting for her because she had the keys. She moved to unlock the door and he didn't step back. Instead he caught her arm and drew her hard against him.

Her eyes jerked open wide as their bodies came in contact. "Nikos!"

"You want this," he told her. "You've been asking for it!"

And he lowered his mouth to hers.

So much for control.

What on earth had she been thinking? How could she have for one minute allowed herself to believe that she could manage what happened when Nikos Costanides touched his lips to hers?

She couldn't. It was as plain and simple as that.

One touch, one taste, and all the good sense and best intentions in the world went right out of her head. She was putty in his hands.

And if she hadn't had one flickering instant's memory of Anita, of Lucy, of Lola, of the lilting Claudia and heaven knew how many other women, there was no telling what a fool she might have made of herself.

They'd driven back to the cottage in silence. She put the car in the garage and handed him back the keys without a word. She didn't look him in the eye. She couldn't.

She would see mockery. Amusement. A playboy's knowing leer.

She hurried back to the house and shut herself in her bedroom.

How was she going to survive this? Nanny to a thirty-two-year-old ladies' man? *Oh, Mari, you fool!*

The first thing she saw was the folder Stavros had given her.

She shouldn't read it. She shouldn't look at anything that might color her view of his older son. It wasn't professional.

And kissing him was?

She glanced sideways at the folder, then curled her fingers into a fist.

The phone rang. She picked it up.

But so had Nikos. It was Claudia again. "Didn't get you up this time, did I?" she said on a voice soft with laughter.

Mari hung up and reached for the folder. The articles all told her what she knew already: that Nikos Costanides was a shallow, irresponsible playboy.

It was the one thing upon which nine out of ten gossip columnists agreed...

CHAPTER FIVE

MARI had never read a lot of tabloid journalism, but she had the notion that very little of it ought to be believed. Still, if even a tenth of what she read was credible, Nikos Costanides was one of the world's sexiest men—with an insatiable appetite for the world's sexiest women.

There didn't seem to be a single actress, model or female recording artist under the age of forty that he hadn't had a fling with. And if those were the ones worthy of being written about, how many hundreds had he bedded who were not?

Heavens.

She read until far into the night. And finally she shoved the folder onto the table unfinished. There was, perhaps, too much punishment here even for her.

She switched off the light and rolled onto her side and told herself not to think about it—about *him.*

Of course she thought about it. She went to sleep and *dreamed* about it. She must have awakened half a dozen times from dreams—or nightmares—in which Nikos kissed, caressed or otherwise touched some of the world's most gorgeous women.

She woke up cranky and out of sorts. Who could blame her? She'd never had dreams like these when she'd been anyone else's nanny!

She tried telling herself that the articles were meaningless—pure hype designed to sell the newspapers or magazines that ran them.

But even if she managed some of the time, Nikos seemed determined to prove that they were true.

Certainly over the next few days he seemed to take great pleasure in flaunting risqué, not-so-*sotto-voce* conversations with a variety of women on the telephone.

There was, of course, the ubiquitous Claudia, still calling at all hours of the day and night. But there were others besides Claudia. In fact, every time Mari came into the living room he was talking or listening to someone of the female persuasion.

Sometimes he was jotting notes on paper and Mari thought he was actually talking business—though she couldn't imagine what because according to the articles he was an unemployed member of the idle rich. But just when she had that notion, he said something like, "Aw, sweetheart, I love it when you say things like that," or, "Oh, pussycat…"

The blatantly seductive tone of his voice set her teeth right on edge. It was as if he was flaunting them in front of her.

Well, fine. Let him.

It wasn't as if she was really interested in him. Not at all. As far as she was concerned, he was just a piece of evidence—living proof, as it were, that she was capable of passion.

He didn't seem capable of anything beyond seductive phone conversations and interminable computer games. Every time he disappeared into his room, talking to Claudia or one of the other women in his life, he seemed to end up sitting on his bed with the laptop, scowling in concentration.

"What a productive existence," Mari jibed, when she brought him lunch one afternoon.

"Huh?" He looked at her, distracted, then rubbed his

eyes, and gave her a bleary ironic smile. "A man's gotta do what a man's gotta do."

And a woman—*this woman*—had merely to survive. She could do that, she assured herself. He was giving her *no* reason to look twice at him. And once he had gone, and she was free of the Costanides men, she could set to work finding the right man to focus her newly discovered passion on.

In the meantime, though, because it was what she was here for, she felt obliged to try to create some sort of rapport between Nikos and his father.

"Talk to him," she urged him. "Listen to him."

But Nikos didn't want to talk, and he didn't want to listen—to her or his father. He turned his back, shrugged her off, ignored her words.

"I'm not interested," he said.

"You are," she argued. She'd seen the look on his face whenever he looked up toward the main house and, especially, when he caught glimpses of Stavros out by the pool with his wife and little boy.

Nikos might think he didn't care, but it was as plain as day that he cared a great deal.

But, "Leave me alone," he said whenever she brought it up.

"I have a headache," he said, almost as often. And, rubbing his temple, he retreated to his room.

Mari thought the headaches might go away if Claudia's interminable middle-of-the-night phone calls went away.

"Doesn't that woman ever sleep?" she groused after four days of being awakened at three o'clock in the morning.

Bleary-eyed and clearly in pain, Nikos shrugged.

'She needs me,'' he said. And he didn't seem to mind. In fact, sometimes Mari heard him calling her!

But this time when the phone rang again, it was someone Nikos called Briana, with a seductive teasing tone that reminded Mari again what a two-timing bastard he was. She gnashed her teeth as, cradling the receiver against his ear, Nikos disappeared into the bedroom.

She should have been glad. After all, she reminded herself, there was no way she could entertain the notion that he was worthy of her interest when he was totally consumed with half the other women on the planet. He must have a little black book the size of the Manhattan phone directory.

"Do you ever date the same woman twice?" she asked him the next night. She didn't want to pretend interest, but the question was out before she could stop it.

He leaned back in his chair and smiled one of his blatantly sexy smiles, though his eyes were still bloodshot from being up most of the night again, and his continual rubbing of his eyes and his temples indicated another headache. "If they're worth it," he said with that easy, teasing smile of his. She could almost hear the smoulder in his voice.

"Is that your way of finding the perfect woman to settle down with?" She knew her tone was sharp, but she couldn't seem to stop that either.

"I'm not settling down. Ever." The seductiveness was gone. Now his tone was just as sharp as hers.

Surprise, surprise. "Too many women in the world to limit yourself to just one?"

"Exactly." He bit the end of the word off, then shoved himself out of his chair. "And I have to go call one now." He started to hobble toward his bedroom.

"It's a little early for Claudia, isn't it?" she asked his back.

"This is Briana," he said without turning. Then, mockingly, he added, "Are you keeping score?"

When the phone rang at a little past three, Mari ignored it. She knew who it was. She had no desire to hear the lovely Claudia again this morning. She rolled over, punched her pillow and said silently to Nikos, *I hope you have the damnedest big headache in the world.*

When it rang again, she said, *Take your time, why don't you?*

And when it shrilled yet again, she yanked the pillow over her head and thought dire thoughts about him and the insomniac Claudia.

Finally, after five rings, it stopped. *About time,* Mari thought. She settled on the pillow again, banishing all thoughts of Nikos bare-legged and bare-chested, having sleepy nocturnal conversations with other women.

There was a tap on her door.

Disoriented, she rolled over, thinking she'd imagined it. Then it came again. "Mari?"

The door opened. Nikos poked his head in. "Do me a favor." His voice sounded rough and edged with pain.

Mari scrambled out of bed and grabbed her robe and pulled it on in the darkness. "Are you all right?"

"Yeah. Just a headache."

"Another one," she growled.

"I'll be fine. But I need to read some figures and I can't seem to focus."

"Figures?" What? They did math problems in the middle of the night? Whatever happened to verbal love-making? Or, for that matter, counting sheep?

"Will you help or not?" He was impatient now.

"Lead on." Shaking her head, she wrapped the robe around her and knotted the tie as she followed him out the door.

He was heading back toward his bedroom as fast as his crutches could take him. By the time she got there, she could just make out his form on his bed. He was lying flat on his back, an arm over his eyes. Beside him lay the phone and the laptop computer.

Nikos kept his arm across his eyes, but gestured toward the computer with his other hand. "Read the figures on that screen into the phone."

Into the phone? Claudia wanted *Mari* to read her a bunch of numbers? What were they doing, comparing Jezzball scores?

"Just sit down, for God's sake," Nikos muttered, and reached out for her hand, pulling her down onto the bed.

Mari sat, but she edged away from him, then fiddled with the angle of the screen, trying to see what numbers he was talking about. There appeared to be a whole row, none of which made any sense to her.

"Hello?" she said tentatively into the phone.

"Hello." A very masculine, albeit British voice startled her in reply. "Brian Jenkin here. I gather Nikos is under the weather at the moment. Don't blame him, he's been working flat out. So if you could just read me the specifications, please?"

Working flat out? Nikos?

She shot Nikos a curious hard stare, but he still had his hand over his eyes. And Brian Jenkin—*Briana?* she wondered. No, it couldn't be! But still—

"Er, yes." Mari fumbled once more with the screen, then slowly, haltingly read down the list of numbers. *M* equaled some number or other. Other letters equaling other amounts. The word *volume* cropped up a lot. It made no sense to her, but, it seemed to satisfy Brian Jenkin.

"Sounds great. Tell him I'll talk to Carruthers and see if this will fly. Or sail, I suppose I should say," Brian said jovially. "Does he want to talk to Carruthers himself?"

Mari relayed the question to Nikos.

"No."

Brian said, "I heard him. That's it, then. Tell him I'll ring back as soon as I've had a word with Carruthers. Thanks a lot." He hung up the phone.

Mari sat with the receiver in her hand, feeling somewhat at sea herself. She looked at the computer screen, at Nikos. She remembered the myriad phone calls, the middle-of-the-night conversations, the soft, seductive, suddenly highly suspicious *"Ah, Briana"*'s breathed into the phone. Her teeth clamped together. A muscle in her temple ticked.

She took a careful measured breath. "He says he'll call you as soon as he's talked to Carruthers."

Nikos grunted. "Thanks."

"How long has this been going on?"

He ran his tongue over his top lip. "Started a few hours ago." His voice was barely more than a whisper.

"I don't mean the headache," Mari said sharply.

He winced. But he didn't answer.

"Briana?" she said sweetly.

The wince became a grimace. Still he didn't talk.

"Who's Claudia?"

He let out a weary exhalation of air. "My secretary."

"Not the one who keeps your little black book straight." Somehow she was sure of that.

"No."

"Who's Brian?" Mari said.

"A friend."

"And business partner," Mari prompted him.

Nikos sighed. "That, too."

"So this playboy thing is an act." It wasn't even a question.

He moved his arm and opened his eyes. "It's not an act," he protested.

"No, I suppose some of it wasn't." She would allow him that much. "You couldn't have possibly conned the world's freest press into reporting a hundred sightings of you and the world's most gorgeous women if there was no kernel of truth. But there's more to you than Nick the Hunk, isn't there?"

"I never said there wasn't."

"You did your damnedest to give that impression."

"It's none of your business what I do."

"Nor your father's?"

"Especially not his!" Nikos propped himself up on his elbows and glared at her. "He never gave a damn about me. He only wants me to do what he tells me to do!"

"And what do you really do?"

There was a pause. "Design boats. And ships."

Mari's eyes grew as big as dinner plates. "*That's* what I was reading to Brian?"

"You were reading conversions for some tankage we had to adjust. Brian is the on-site coordinator. In Cornwall. That's where we're based."

"The three a.m. phone calls?"

Nikos grimaced. "It's eight in Cornwall. He works on his time—and when he needs me, I do, too."

"This is a...big business?"

"Yes." And somehow that wasn't a surprise, either.

"Have you been doing it long?"

"Why? Do you want references? Want me to design you a ship?" he snapped. "I'm out of your price range."

"Undoubtedly. But I'm still curious. Why would you bother to keep a perfectly respectable career hidden?"

His jaw tightened. "Because I choose to."

"You want to be thought of as a playboy."

"I never said I was a playboy."

"But—"

"And you're not telling the old man about this."

"But he'd— "

"*No!*" His fingers tightened so hard around her wrist that she thought he would cut off the circulation. Experimentally she wiggled her fingers. It seemed to make him aware of the pressure he was exerting. He dropped her hand. "Sorry. But I don't want you to tell him." Dark, pain-filled eyes bored into hers.

Mari nodded slowly. "I won't."

He sank back and shut his eyes again. His chest heaved slightly, then he breathed more easily.

"You're a naval architect?" Mari asked after a moment. "How did that happen?" It wasn't something a person just fell into.

"I always messed about in boats. Goes with the genes, I suppose." His mouth twisted bitterly. "Costanides men have been involved with boats in one way or another as long as anyone can remember. I had a boat when I was a kid. Sailing was my...salvation." His face relaxed a little in reflection. "I liked drawing them, designing them, too—as well as sailing them." He shrugged. "Nobody tried to tell me how to do that."

"Nobody like Stavros?"

"He was very big at trying to tell me what to do. Wanted me to do things his way. Work in his business. Study what he told me to."

Play The *Lucky Hearts* Game

and get... FREE BOOKS, a FREE GIFT... and MUCH more!

Yes! I have scratched off the silver card. Please send me my **2 FREE BOOKS** and **FREE MYSTERY GIFT**. I understand that I am under no obligation to purchase any books as explained on the back of this card.

Scratch Here!
then look below to see what
your cards get you...

306 HDL CNFQ

106 HDL CNFP

Name _____
(PLEASE PRINT)

Address _____ Apt.# _____

City _____ State/Prov. _____ Zip/Postal Code _____

Twenty-one gets you
2 FREE BOOKS and a
FREE MYSTERY GIFT!

Twenty gets you
2 FREE BOOKS!

Nineteen gets you
1 FREE BOOK!

TRY AGAIN!

If offer card is missing write to: Harlequin Reader Service, 3010 Walden Ave., P.O. Box 1867, Buffalo NY 14240-1867

BUSINESS REPLY MAIL
FIRST-CLASS MAIL   PERMIT NO. 717   BUFFALO, NY

POSTAGE WILL BE PAID BY ADDRESSEE

HARLEQUIN READER SERVICE
3010 WALDEN AVE
PO BOX 1867
BUFFALO NY 14240-9952

NO POSTAGE
NECESSARY
IF MAILED
IN THE
UNITED STATES

And he wouldn't have gone along with any of it, she could see that. A boy like Nikos, whose father had left him, would never respect that father enough to do what he wanted.

"'Go to Greece,' he said. 'Or go to Harvard,'" Nikos went on. "'Learn the old family way. Learn the new Harvard Business School way.' I wasn't interested. I didn't want Greece or Harvard. I went to Glasgow."

"Scotland?"

"They taught what I wanted to learn."

"Naval architecture."

"Yes. But he didn't know that. He never asked. He just said that if I didn't do what he wanted, he wouldn't foot the bills. I could waste my life as far as he was concerned." He opened his eyes and looked at her again. "So as far as he is concerned, I have."

And Mari knew that was the whole reason for Nikos's playboy façade right there.

If Stavros didn't care enough to find out who his son really was, if he only thought of Nikos as an extension of him, Nikos would solve the problem his own way. A typically in-your-face Costanides way. *Let the old man think I'm wasting my life. Let him fret. Let him stew. He doesn't want me, I don't want him.*

"And that was that?"

"Not quite. He demanded that I come work for him in the summer—to learn the business, not because he wanted me around. I went, even though I didn't want to, because my mother asked me to. 'You'll get to know each other better,' she told me." Nikos gave a bitter laugh. "I never saw him. He put me in some damned smelly warehouse in Athens one year, and the next he stuck me in an airless office building in the Bronx where I spent eight hours a day filling out forms. The next year

I had a chance to work on a design project. I wanted to do that. He threw some nonsense at me about only wanting to play, never wanting to work.'' His fists clenched around the sheet and he had to consciously loosen his fingers.

''And that's when you decided to let him think what he wanted.''

''He already thought what he wanted. He always has.'' He shut his eyes and sighed. ''So now you know.''

Mari sat quietly, studying the complex man lying just inches from her. She saw the sexy playboy, the intense designer, the hurt child. They were all there, tangled up inside one tough, hard-edged man.

She sighed softly, too. ''Now I know.''

He'd blown his cover.

He remembered that the minute he opened his eyes and saw the computer back on the desk where it belonged and not in the bed where he seemed to have had it most of the time over the past few days.

He sighed and rubbed a hand over his eyes. They were what had finally betrayed him. All the hours squinting at the screen had done exactly what the doctor had told him they would do.

''Strain and stress will cause you headaches. Head injuries take time to heal,'' he'd said the last time Nikos went in, complaining. ''Give it a rest.''

But he couldn't give it a rest when work needed to be done.

Finally, though, he couldn't even focus on the work he'd done. When Brian had called, needing the answers, he'd needed them right then. There was no time for Nikos to say he'd call back in a few hours when the lines sorted themselves out and the numbers made sense again.

So he'd had to get Mari to read them. And of course Mari knew she wasn't reading the scores of some computer game.

Now what?

He didn't know. He dared hope she wouldn't tell his father, though he supposed it wouldn't matter much if she did. The pleasure he'd got out of convincing the old man that his oldest son was a worthless, lazy ladies' man had waned some time ago.

Now keeping up the façade was just a matter of principle.

The phone rang, and he noticed that it was out of reach as well. He sighed and started to haul himself up to get it, but it stopped ringing almost at once. If he was very quiet, he could hear Mari talking in the living room.

To Stavros?

Maybe. He didn't care.

To her aunts? Possibly. He wondered about them. Were they like her? She'd told him a few days ago that they raised her after her parents had died. That explained a lot of her more nunlike tendencies. He'd said that just to watch her blush, and he'd been gratified when she had.

"I had other influences in my life, too," she'd told him seriously. "My uncle Arthur was a dancing instructor. He had quite a way with the ladies. Though he was not," she'd added, "quite as proficient as you."

He wondered what she thought about his proficiency now.

She knew who Claudia was. She knew that all those phone calls from "Briana" were really Brian with business problems. There had been women who had called him over the past few days. Lucy had called. So had her sister, Lola. But not as many as he'd made it seem. He'd played it up, teased them, made sure Mari had heard.

So she'd think what his father thought. So she'd cross him off as a hopeless womanizer.

And now?

Now there was a light tap and door opened a crack. Mari peeked in . "Oh, you are awake. Good. Brian's on the phone. He wants you to know that Carruthers is pleased." There was a hint of a smile on her face. "For the moment," she added with an almost impish grin.

Seeing it, Nikos permitted a hint of a smile to touch his lips. Something in him seemed to loosen, to lighten. Not only because he'd satisfied Carruthers, though that was certainly worth celebrating.

Mari knew. He'd thought he would be sorry.

Instead he was relieved.

She was out of her depth, out of her league, over her head.

It would have been better by far if he'd been the womanizing playboy he'd pretended to be.

It had made sense to fight her attraction to a man who had a woman in every port. It hadn't been easy to resist Nikos Costanides's charm when she'd been sure he laid it on so freely, but it had been easier than it was now.

He *did* lay it on freely, she reminded herself. Even naval architects with clients and demands and a secretary named Claudia could be charming! *Remember Nita, and Lucy, and all those women in the magazines and newspaper?*

But that wasn't the *real* Nikos. Or certainly not the *whole* Nikos. That was the public Nikos—the one he had created to irritate his father.

That was the Nikos who had kissed her the first day when she'd knocked on his door. She understood that. And she could resist him. She had been resisting him since she'd been here.

The question was, which Nikos had kissed her beside the car the day they'd gone to Montauk?

There hadn't been any photographers there then. There hadn't been any journalists. Not even any interested witnesses. It had happened just between the two of them.

She and...*which Nikos?*

She tried to tell herself it didn't really matter. *Whichever* Nikos it was, she couldn't handle him. Didn't *want* to handle him. It was her passion she needed to develop and control—not the man who'd inspired it. Passion was a transferrable commodity.

At least she told herself that. And hoped.

She should have run.

She didn't have the chance.

She took the call from Brian and received his misplaced congratulations—as if *she'd* had anything to do with their success beyond reading the numbers on the screen. Then she went to see if Nikos could talk to him.

He had fallen asleep soon after they'd hung up the phone after talking to Brian in the middle of the night. She'd got some pain medication down him, then wordlessly rubbed his temples and the back of his neck, trying to ease what strain she could.

She hadn't known if it would help, but when she'd quit before he fell asleep, he'd muttered, "Don't stop," and so she'd started again.

When at last he had gone to sleep, she'd slipped out of the room to her own. But not before she'd stood and looked at him, traced his features, softened only slightly by sleep, and remembered the feel of his lips on hers.

The feel—the passion—she would do her damnedest to transfer to another man. A safer man.

The memory of Nikos—well, she just wanted that for herself.

Now she waited until he finished talking to Brian, then she said, "I'll turn in my notice."

He frowned. "What? Why?"

"You obviously don't need 'shaping up.' And I..." She didn't think there was any way she could tell him the rest.

In any case, he didn't give her the chance. He said, "No."

"What do you mean, no? That's what you've wanted all along! To get rid of me, to turn your back on your father—"

"I still don't give a damn about my father," he said. "But I don't want you to go."

Her foolish heart leapt for just a moment. Then she steeled herself against any such feelings. "Why?"

"Because I could use your help for one thing. Brian and I have been working on designs for a shipper. It's a big contract. Not just in terms of money, but in terms of reputation. For the company, not me. I'm a pretty silent partner. Brian deals with the customers, does the on-site stuff, and I stay at home, take the specs he gives me and work on the actual design. Some people are easier to please than others. Some people let you do it your way as long as you give them what they want. The guy we're working with now has a mind of his own. And he changes it frequently as you've seen," Nikos added grimly. "I've been trying to accommodate all his suggestions and all the things he says he needs. And every time I get them figured out, they change again. That's why all the phone calls. We've got other customers, too, though. Other designs that need to be worked on. And I don't have time to field all Brian's calls and read him stuff when I should be working on other projects. *Anyone* can read him the stuff I've come up with."

"Me," Mari translated, trying not to feel deflated. After all, she didn't *want* him to want her, did she?

Nikos nodded. "Yes. Can you type?"

"Of course."

"Even better."

"But—" Mari shook her head. "I work for your father."

"So go right ahead. Look." Nikos leaned forward earnestly. "He tricked you into this, right? I don't know what he did to make you stay, but he must have done something so that you couldn't—or wouldn't—walk the minute you realized you weren't dealing with a four-year-old. Right again?" He waited for her reluctant nod. "So, fine. You stay, you're fulfilling your obligation to him."

"I'm not teach—"

"Not teaching me respect?" His gaze narrowed. "I have a lot of respect for people who earn it, Mari Lewis."

Yes, she supposed he did.

"It wouldn't be honest."

"There's nothing to stop you *trying* to teach me to respect him," Nikos pointed out, though his smile told her it was damned unlikely that her efforts would bear fruit. "I'll pay you."

"I'm already being paid. I can't take your money."

"Give the old man his back when we're done."

"And when would that be?"

"When I get my cast off I'm leaving. I told you that. I'll go to Cornwall where Brian is. That's where we build—in a shipyard in Falmouth. Then Brian will be able to get at me in a zone where it's daytime for both of us."

"A few days, in other words?" Was she terrible to be considering it? Did she have any real choice?

Nikos dipped his dark head. "As you say. A few days."

"And you won't...you won't..." Instinctively and unintentionally she pressed her hand against her mouth again. She could remember the touch of his mouth as if it had just been there.

"Kiss you?" Nikos finished for her. "Only if you want me to." A hint of the wickedest grin in the world touched his mouth. Then, quite suddenly, it faded and the look on his face became serious. "*Do* you want me to?"

She shook her head vehemently, then abruptly she stopped at the realization that there was one part of her that *did* want him doing it again.

Honesty, she always told the children she cared for, was the best policy. For the first time she really doubted that. But the habit was deeply ingrained. "I liked it when you kissed me," she admitted, not looking at him. "And I liked kissing you, but—"

"But kissing for you has to do with love and marriage and commitment?" He said the words almost harshly.

Mari nodded. She slanted a glance in his direction. The look on his face was unreadable. His dark eyes were hooded. One of his fists was white-knuckled as he gripped a handful of the sheet.

"It doesn't mean that for me," he told her.

"It could—" Oh, heavens! What was she saying?

He shook his head. "No. I won't let it. I don't want it!"

And she did.

A corner of Nikos's mouth lifted in rueful acknowledgement of their quandary. Then he pressed his lips together. "I have, despite what the tabloids might say, a certain amount of self-control. And I really could use your help until I get this cast off. If you change your mind," he added hopefully, "you feel free to tell me. But if that's the way you want it, Mari Lewis, I won't be kissing you again."

CHAPTER SIX

SO SHE stayed.

And if her conscience bothered her whenever Stavros rang up to demand a report, she took solace in the fact that she could tell him quite honestly that she and Nikos were getting along, that he was talking to her, that they seemed to be on the same wavelength.

This last might have been stretching it a bit. But over the next three days she really did find herself getting attuned to Nikos's work habits and thought patterns.

Maybe it was an instinctive rapport that grew up between them because she had grown up sailing boats, too. She didn't know the first thing about tankage and impact resistance, and some kind of density or other that seemed to be giving him headaches figuratively as well as literally, but these were *boats* he was talking about, figuring about, worrying about—even in the abstract—and as such she was interested.

Or maybe she was just interested in him.

She discounted that, of course. She didn't want to think about the chemistry that existed between herself and Nikos Costanides! If he could put it aside for the best interests of his business, so could *she!*

That's what she told herself. For the most part, that's what she did.

But the awareness was still there.

Sometimes, to get away from it, she would leave him working and go up to the pool and swim or play with Alexander and talk to Julietta, who was seven months into a difficult pregnancy and was happy to have someone else to talk to and to chase Alexander around.

She did her best to avoid Stavros. For all his obtuseness when it came to dealing with his son, he was surprisingly astute in other ways. She thought he might well manage to worm some hint of Nikos's occupation out of her. Especially because she would have really liked to tell him.

"I don't see why you won't tell him," she said to Nikos more than once. "It would make all the difference."

"Yes," Nikos agreed drily, "it would."

Which, she understood from the silence that followed, was exactly why he wasn't. It was a matter of pride. And if Stavros was a proud, stubborn man, Nikos had more pride than anyone she knew.

So Mari didn't say a word. Even though she was working for Stavros, her allegiance was to his son. It would have been that way even if Nikos were really four years old. Though the parent footed the bills, a nanny's first commitment was to the child.

Even if the child was thirty-two!

They worked well together. That was the good news. The bad news, as far as Mari was concerned, was that, now that he felt no need to hide his career from her, she liked him even more.

She saw the serious, dedicated side of Nikos Costanides that he kept well hidden from his father and the rest of the world. She saw the way he tackled the problems Brian called with and spent hours, literally, working them out, trying first one thing and then another. He was dedicated, tenacious, determined.

Everything she admired in a man.

Except that he wanted nothing to do with commitment. And therefore, realistically, he wanted nothing to do with her.

That didn't stop him looking at her, though. It didn't stop the leisurely wander of his gaze when they were working together. It didn't stop him licking his lips sometimes or sighing and shaking his head.

She knew what he was thinking!

If the truth was known, she was thinking it, too!

But she had to resist. Getting involved with Nikos Costanides would be a one-way trip to misery. He didn't want what she wanted. He wanted to make love, not really love.

And so sometimes, when the wanting got too obvious and her own good intentions got particularly feeble, she took herself off to the pool.

The breeze off the ocean kept things cool most of the day, and the water kept Alexander occupied when he didn't have a friend over to play.

Mari thought Julietta could have used some help at this point in her pregnancy. But Julietta was as stubborn as the rest of the Costanides family. "Angelika raised Nikos by herself," she'd told Mari early in their acquaintance. "Stavros thought it was a good thing."

Mari was surprised that Julietta, and Stavros for that matter, measured the way to raise a child by the way Nikos had been raised, but she had merely nodded and smiled. "Well, if you ever need a little rest, give me a call," she'd said. "I'm sure Nikos won't mind sparing me for a while."

Exactly what Stavros had told his wife about her living with Nikos, Mari was never sure. And Julietta never said. She seemed to take it for granted that Mari was there to help Nikos. That she'd been a nanny seemed beside the point, and Mari had never spelled it out for her.

This afternoon Julietta was resting on a chaise longue and Alexander was playing alone in the shallow end of the pool when Mari walked up to join them.

"Is Nikos taking another nap?" Julietta asked when Mari got close enough to talk.

"He doesn't need me right now." Mari didn't want to lie and she wasn't about to say that Nikos was on the phone arguing with Brian. The variable Mr. Carruthers had handed down some more modifications this morning, after Nikos had worked most of yesterday trying to accommodate the last set.

This time when Brian called, he had blown sky-high. Mari did her best to soothe him, but he wasn't in the mood for soothing. "There's only one thing that would soothe me," he told her sharply—and the way his gaze drifted down her body, she didn't have to ask what it was.

"You said you wouldn't even kiss—" she began.

"I know what I said," Nikos retorted between clenched teeth. "So if you don't want me going back on my word, get out of here now and leave me to this."

Mari left.

"I'm soooo bored," Julietta said now. "I feel like a beached whale or a pregnant hippo." She rubbed her distended abdomen and sighed.

"Maybe it would be good for you to go in the pool. The water could help you support the baby."

"Maybe," Julietta agreed. "But I can't as long as it's just me here with Alex. He tries to be careful, but he forgets he can't leap on me these days."

"I'll go in with you."

Julietta's eyes lit up with gratitude. "Oh, would you

mind? That would be wonderful.'' She eased her ungainly body to a sitting position and, with Mari's help, hauled herself to her feet. ''I'm so swollen,'' she said, craning her neck to look down in an effort to see her feet and ankles. ''Much more this time than with Alex.''

''Every baby's different, they say.'' Mari took her arm so Julietta wouldn't slip on the wet tiles.

''Well, I'll be glad to get this one out of me and on its way.'' Julietta made a face. ''Alex, at least, was a winter baby.'' She smiled at her dark-haired son, who was jumping up and down in the water in eagerness as he watched her come down the steps into the pool.

''Are you comin' swimming with me, Mommy?'' Alex was bouncing on his toes.

''How about if Mommy swims on her own and you swim alongside with me,'' Mari suggested.

Alex looked at her warily. He wasn't exactly shy with other people, but he was definitely reserved, as if he was going to do some serious study before he made up his mind about anyone. A lot like his brother, Mari thought.

She'd told Nikos yesterday at dinner how much his half-brother was like him.

''Don't tell the old man that,'' Nikos had said promptly. Then his face had split in a grin. ''On second thought, do. It'll drive him nuts.''

In fact, Mari didn't know how Stavros would react to the idea. She knew he was deeply devoted to his little son. She suspected he was equally devoted to the older one—but had no idea how to show it. He couldn't play catch with Nikos or throw him up in the air or give him rides on his shoulders in the pool.

Had he ever done any of those things with Nikos? she wondered. But one look at Nikos's hard closed expression, and she had known better than to ask.

"What do you say?" she asked Alex now. "Shall we swim alongside your mom?"

He chewed on his fingernail. "Mmm. Yeah, I guess. Or we could race her!"

Mari slipped down into the water. "Come here, then."

She felt Alex's small eager hands grip her shoulders, and she put her hands behind her, giving him a boost so that he could wrap his legs around her torso and his arms across her neck. "Okay. Here we go. Watch out, Mom." She grinned at Julietta, by this time submerged till only her head and shoulders were out of the water. "Better get going or we'll catch you."

"Oh, you will, will you?" Julietta began a lazy breaststroke toward the far end of the pool. Mari started after her.

At first Alex was content just to ride. But as his mother got further ahead, the Costanides competitive spirit won out.

"C'mon, Mari!" he yelled, kicking her like a pony. "Catch her!" He wriggled and bounced, digging his heels even harder into her sides as if that would make her go faster. It slowed her down and they began to fall behind.

"No!" he wailed in dismay. "We're gonna *lose!*"

Then Julietta, bless her, slowed a little, and Mari and Alex surged past.

"We won! Mari an' me won!" Alex crowed.

"Oh, good for you!" Julietta beamed at her son. "Thank you," she mouthed to Mari.

"My pleasure," Mari mouthed back. Then she said, "Come on, Alex. Let's swim back to the other end and you can show me how well you swim on your own."

Alex went with her eagerly, not kicking this time. "You're living with Nikos."

"I'm helping him," Mari corrected him, but she supposed from the boy's point of view, he was right, too.

"He's my brother."

"I know."

Alex made swishy fish movements with his hands. "He doesn't like me."

Mari looked at him, startled. "He doesn't? How do you know that."

Alex lifted narrow shoulders. "He doesn't talk to me. He just walks away. An' he never smiles."

"I think he has important things on his mind," Mari said.

"Maybe." But he didn't sound convinced. He sounded forlorn. Mari wondered if Nikos knew that Alex noticed—and cared.

She gave the boy's small hand a squeeze. "I think Nikos likes you, Alex. But he hasn't had a lot of experience with little boys."

"How come? He used to be one," Alex said.

Out of the mouths of babes. "Well, yes, but that was a long time ago. Sometimes when they grow up, big boys forget."

"Maybe it's 'cause he hit his head. Nikos had a accident, you know. He was hurt bad. My daddy said he might die."

"Your daddy told *you* that?"

Alex ducked his head. "I was listenin'. He said it to my mom."

"I think your daddy was really worried about Nikos right after the accident," Mari said carefully. "But he doesn't have to worry now, and neither do you. Nikos didn't die then, and he's not going to die now."

"You sure?" Alex's brown eyes, so like his brother's, searched hers.

Mari gave the little boy a hug. "I'm sure."

Julietta thanked her again profusely when she came out of the pool. "I know other mothers cope wonderfully well without any help at all," she said ruefully. "But I have been so tired these last couple of weeks. And now that Stavros is gone..."

"Stavros is gone?"

"He had to go to Athens," Julietta explained. "He'll be home next week."

By next week, Nikos would be out of his cast and gone. Mari wondered if Stavros realized that. She wondered what he'd say to her when he came back and found Nikos had left.

"He works so hard," Julietta said. "He ought to slow down. He had a heart attack two years ago, you know. I...hope you can convince Nikos to come back into the firm. It would be so much better."

For Stavros, Mari wanted to say.

And for Nikos?

She didn't know.

"Alex thinks you don't like him," she told Nikos that night.

He was lying on the bed with his eyes shut. He'd been working all afternoon with some CAD program that was going to save his business and ruin his head, he told Mari. She forced another dose of the pain medication down him. "Rest," she commanded.

"I can't. Not until I tell Carruthers what I think of him," he muttered.

"I'll do that for you. Lie down and dictate."

He flashed a grin at her. "To you, sweetheart? I'd be delighted."

Mari flushed. "You promised not to do that!"

"No. I promised not to kiss you. I didn't say I wouldn't flirt."

So to change the subject, she told him what Alex had said.

Nikos lifted one brow. "Don't like him? I never have anything to do with him."

"I think that's the whole point. He'd like to have something to do with you."

"Tell that to the old man. He makes damn good and sure Alex is never around when I am. Doesn't want me contaminating him."

"Oh, I doubt that."

But Nikos didn't, it was clear.

The next morning she went back to the big house to see if perhaps she could give Julietta a break and, incidentally, find out what Stavros's second wife thought.

Julietta was feeling a little better this morning, and she suggested they walk down to the beach. They did, and while Alex played in the sand Mari brought the subject up. "Nikos says Stavros won't permit Alex to come to the cottage."

Julietta pursed her lips. "I think 'won't permit' is a little strong."

"But he does discourage Alex from going down to see Nikos?"

Julietta scooped up a handful of sand and let it trickle through her fingers. "I think he's afraid that Nikos's resentment will hurt Alex."

"Nikos resents his father, not Alex."

"Yes. And I wouldn't blame him, I guess. Stavros wasn't the father to Nikos that he has been to Alex. He had to work so hard back then," she explained earnestly. "To make the business a success, to justify his marriage."

Mari's brows drew together at this last. "What do you mean, to justify his marriage?"

"Angelika was the daughter of a very wealthy family, and she was supposed to marry someone else. She was *promised* by her father to someone else. But she loved Stavros, and her father finally gave in." Julietta sighed and shook her head. "I think Stavros always felt he *had* to be a success so he could prove he was worthy of her."

Mari digested that. She had assumed that the marriage was arranged. She hadn't assumed that Angelika had loved Stavros. Not at first anyway. Later—well, Nikos had agreed she'd loved him then.

When she went back to the cottage, she tried to ask Nikos about it. But he wouldn't discuss his father and mother in the same breath.

"Worthy of her?" He nearly spat. "He *wasn't* worthy of her!"

And that was that.

The phone rang then.

"Damn it! Doesn't Brian ever sleep?" Nikos muttered.

"I'll get it," Mari said. But it wasn't Brian at all. It was her aunt Em.

"We've missed you, dear. Are you coming this week? Are you bringing little Nikos?"

"It's my day off," Mari protested. And he wasn't *little* Nikos! Nor was she about to bring him!

"But we love to meet your little charges," Aunt Em said wistfully. "You know how lonely we get out here now that Bett doesn't drive anymore."

"Well, I—"

"We'd watch him," her aunt assured her. "You could have your rest."

"I don't need rest exactly, but—"

"His parents wouldn't approve?"

Mari hesitated. There was no way, of course, that she was taking Nikos out there. But maybe she could take Alex. It would be good for Julietta to have a little time to herself. And it would be equally good for her aunts. And she really didn't need a day off that badly.

"I'll see," she said. "But remember, his name is Alex, not Nikos."

When she hung up, Mari turned back to Nikos. "It was my aunt. Tomorrow's my day off," she explained, "and they'd like me to come. I thought maybe I could take Alex with me..."

A grin quirked his mouth. "Not me?"

Mari shook her head. "Definitely not you."

He managed to look crestfallen. Then he grinned. "Pity. I'd like to meet the women who raised you."

"And I *wouldn't* like them to meet you."

"You don't think I've behaved myself this week?"

"Of course you have. Sort of," she qualified. "But..."

"I think we've done very well." He grimaced. "And it hasn't been easy."

Mari's eyes widened. She felt a hint of color bloom on her cheeks. He was still interested, then? In spite of not wanting to be?

"Good thing I'm leaving," he said.

"What?" She felt her whole body tense. "When?"

"Tomorrow. I'm getting the cast off in the afternoon."

"Tomorrow?" He'd never said that! Had never even mentioned it!

"The nurse called this morning while you were at the beach. Said they had a cancellation. Wondered if I wanted it. I said yes. Twenty-four more hours and I'll be gone."

And not a moment too soon.

He'd had all he could do these past few days to keep his hands off Mari Lewis. It was all well and good to say he wasn't going to kiss her again, to tell her he was keeping his hands off unless she invited him to do otherwise, of course, to tell himself that he was doing the sane, sensible thing—hell, even *honorable*—by keeping their relationship on a completely professional footing.

It was something else again to get to sleep at night.

He didn't *want* to be sleeping at night. He wanted to be in bed with Mari Lewis doing what God intended men and women to do—and enjoying every minute of it.

Instead he was tossing and turning in his wide empty bed, alone, with visions of ship's tanks and Mari Lewis chasing each other through his brain. It had been like that every night since she'd been here. It was no wonder his damned head ached!

His head wasn't the only thing either.

And watching Mari Lewis nibble on a strand of her hair, watching her tip her head and lick her lips when she was tasting dinner, watching her sashay down the hall wearing that stupid robe that simply accentuated all her curves, was making it worse.

He needed relief. He needed out.

So this morning he'd called the doctor and asked for his earliest appointment. The sooner he was free of the cast, the sooner he would be free of a lot of things that ailed him.

Tomorrow, he promised himself.

Less than twenty-four hours and he would be in Cornwall, sorting out Brian, taking on Carruthers face-to-face, getting his life back.

Mostly he would be free of his father—and Mari Lewis.

Julietta was thrilled at Mari's suggestion that she take Alex to visit her aunts. "If you wouldn't mind," she added hesitantly. "I know you're supposed to be with Nikos."

"Nikos has a doctor's appointment," Mari said. "And he arranged for Thomas to take him." He'd informed her of that this morning.

"But I'd—" But she hadn't finished her sentence. If he didn't want her accompanying him, he didn't want her. And that was that. She wasn't going to beg.

Something in her expression must have said that because Nikos grimaced slightly. "It's better this way," he said.

"So we'll say goodbye now," Mari replied after a moment.

"Yes."

Their eyes met. He reached out a hand and took one of hers. It was a touch she'd longed for, but until his fingers wrapped hers, she hadn't realized just how much. She tried to fight the feeling, but it was useless.

"Bye," she said softly. She flicked a glance up at him, but couldn't hold it.

"Bye." But he didn't let her hand go. He squeezed it lightly, his fingers tightening over hers, linking them for just a moment. Then, "Mari?"

She blinked and managed to meet his gaze.

He tipped his head, a corner of his mouth lifted. "How about just one...for the road?"

She should have said no. *Of course she should have said no.*

She didn't. She couldn't. One for the road. One to remember him by. One kiss by the real Nikos Costanides.

She ran her tongue lightly over her lips and gave a quick almost jerky nod of her head. Then she lifted her face, offering her mouth. Bracing herself.

"It won't hurt," he whispered as he loosed her hand and brought his up to cup the back of her neck and hold her. Then he touched his lips to hers.

His kiss was warm, gentle. Tender. It wasn't at all like the first kiss he'd given her. It was everything like the second. It taught her as nothing else could exactly which Nikos Costanides had been kissing her that day. It made her feel alive, eager, hungry. It spoke of longing and desire and passion.

And she answered with longing and desire and passion of her own. She answered with her heart. And she heard a harsh aching sound come from somewhere deep inside him.

Then he stepped back, breathing heavily, raggedly, and just looked at her.

Mari looked back.

Then he said roughly, "Go on."

And she went. But she went knowing he was wrong. He'd said it wouldn't hurt.

It did.

Taking Alex to visit her aunts was the best thing she could have done.

He was all eyes and ears. Bouncing. Talkative. Eager.

She had once thought there was nothing as distracting as a four-year-old when it came to keeping you from thinking about anything else but him.

That was the case with Alex. And a good thing, too.

If she hadn't had Alex to deal with, she'd have thought too much about Nikos. As it was, she had no time.

"Look! A sailboat!" He pointed one out on the horizon. "Do your aunts got a sailboat?"

"A small one."

Alex looked at her with shining eyes. "Can we go sailing? Please, Mari! Please?"

At the sight of his eager face, she understood all too well how some parents got sucked into promising more than they could deliver. "We'll see."

Aunt Em and Aunt Bett wouldn't be up to going sailing. But maybe she could make time, after she'd paid the bills and finished talking to the bank manager. She'd always loved to sail. Uncle Arthur used to call it "her passion." Once upon a time she'd thought that sailing was all she had a passion for. Before Nikos.

Everything she did that day seemed to come back to Nikos.

She was almost grateful for the bills to pay, and the nagging credit manager to placate, and the books to go over. Except the rows of figures reminded her of Nikos. And the little boy following her aunts around and chattering reminded her of Nikos. And the sight of the sea reminded her of Nikos. And—

There was no end to her thoughts of Nikos.

It was almost a relief to finish the bills and have Alex come into the dining room with a plate of the cookies he and the aunts had made, begging her, "Can we go sailing now?"

"Yes," Mari said. "Let's." She could use the exercise. Perhaps it would *exorcise* the man in her mind. At least she and Nikos had never gone sailing.

"Nikos has a sailboat," Alex told her as he skipped alongside her down to the dock. "He's a *good* sailor. My daddy says so. They used to go sailing when Nikos was little."

That was interesting. He'd never mentioned sailing with his father at all. "Do you sail with your daddy?"

Alex shook his head. "Nope. He only goed with Nikos. But maybe if I knew something, he'd take me," he added, brightening just a bit.

So Mari taught him how to cast off, how to put up the sail. She took him out on the water and, catching a cross wind, pointed the boat toward the house, then put Alex's hand on the tiller.

"Here," she said, "aim for Aunt Em on the dock."

"M-me aim? Me sail." His eyes went round and wide as he looked at Mari. He held the tiller in a death grip.

"You. Easy there," Mari said. "Yes, like that." She kept her hand near his as they moved quickly toward where Aunt Em stood, watching. Alex, his arm almost rigid with his determination to do it right, reminded her of Nikos when he was hunched over his figures, trying to get them perfect.

Don't, she admonished herself. *Don't think about him.*

She tried not to. When they got close to the dock, she said, "All right. My turn," and she tacked and brought the boat around so they were headed toward the point. "Your turn again."

Eagerly Alex took hold once more and, catching his tongue between his lips, he pointed the boat in the direction she indicated. This time he relaxed a little, eased up on his grip, actually breathed a couple of times. The first time she thought he hadn't!

"Good job," she said. "Wonderful. I think you're a born sailor, Alex."

"Do you?" he asked eagerly, and the grin he gave her was Nikos when all his figures were perfect.

They didn't stay out long. Short and sweet, Mari believed, was the best way to teach anybody anything. *"Leave 'em wanting more,"* Aunt Bett had always said. It was clear that Alex still wanted more when she tacked once more and said, "Enough for now. Back to Aunt Em."

"Awwww," Alex moaned. Then, "I can come again, can't I?" he pleaded.

"I hope so," Mari said. Though exactly where she would be standing with regard to the Costanides family after Nikos left today remained to be seen.

Maybe, she thought, Stavros would keep her on to help with Alex while Julietta took care of their new baby. Certainly Julietta's desire to take care of her own children was admirable, but where was the harm in having a little help?

And if she stayed on to help care for Alex, perhaps she would see Nikos.

Ah, Mari, don't even think about it.

"Didja see us?" Alex asked, almost leaping out of the boat when they reached the dock where Aunt Em and Aunt Bett waited. "Didja see me sailing?"

"Indeed we did. You did very well." Aunt Em gave him a hug.

"My, yes. You're a natural sailor, I would say," Aunt Bett concurred.

Alex beamed. "That's what Mari said."

"Well, Mari's right. Now come along and let's see

what a natural you are in the kitchen. You can help me peel potatoes for supper."

Alex looked at her wide-eyed. "Me?"

"Of course, dear." Aunt Bett held out a hand to him. "All good sailors peel potatoes."

Alex went off with them, an aunt on either hand, and left Mari to finish with the boat. She lowered the sail and took it off, then began to fold it, trying not to dream about staying on with Alex, about maybe seeing Nikos again.

It would be far better, she knew, if she *never* saw him again!

"Mari!"

She jerked and spun around, startled. *"Nikos?"* Here? Indeed he was.

As if her foolish longing had conjured him up, he was limping down the steps toward her. He no longer had a cast on. He no longer used crutches. But he probably should have, because he was moving so fast and so precariously that he looked as if he might fall over.

Mari hurried toward him. "I thought you'd left!"

"I was leaving. But Julietta was having contractions. I've taken her to the hospital!"

CHAPTER SEVEN

HE SHOULD never have stopped at the house.

If he hadn't, he wouldn't have known. He wouldn't have seen Julietta's white face, wouldn't have heard the panicky quaver in her voice when she told him she was having contractions, that she thought she was having the baby.

"You can't be!" he'd said, as if he could somehow stop it just by command. As if he'd been able to command anything to do his bidding of late.

"I am," Julietta said miserably. "They've been getting worse all day."

"Did you call the doctor?"

She shook her head. "I didn't think it was going to happen. I'm not due for two months."

"Tell that to the kid," Nikos said harshly. "Come on. Get on the couch. Lie down."

He took her arm and steered her in that direction. It wasn't easy. He didn't have good balance since they'd taken the cast off. He had an orthopedic shoe contraption that made him feel like he was stumbling every time he took a step. He *really* felt like he was stumbling now.

What the hell was he supposed to do with his pregnant *stepmother*, for heaven's sake? Getting involved with his father's new family was the last thing he wanted to do.

"Where's the old man?" he'd asked harshly.

"Stavros is in Athens," Julietta said faintly. She put her feet up on the couch and looked up at him as if he could somehow conjure up her husband.

"Figures," Nikos snapped. Stavros was never around when he was needed. That, at least, hadn't changed. "Have you called him?"

"I can't...f-find him."

"What do you mean, you can't find him?"

"He was having some sort of top-flight meeting with a company he's thinking of buying. He said it was all hush-hush. He didn't tell me where he was going to be."

"Of all the idiotic—" Words failed him.

"Oh, Nikos!" She wrapped her arms around her middle. "Here it comes again."

Nikos swore. Then he called the doctor. Then he called the hospital. The doctor said he'd meet her there. The hospital said to bring her right in.

"Me?" Nikos said.

Who else?

It wasn't his job. It was Stavros's job! But Stavros was halfway around the world.

"Poor Stavros," Julietta murmured as he bundled her into his car. "It'll be just like last time."

Nikos didn't know what the hell she meant by that. Had the old man been on the other side of the earth when Alex was born, too?

He got her to the hospital in record time. He handed her over to the nurses and turned to go. "I'll call Adrianos and see if he can find the old man," he said.

She nodded weakly. "And Alex. You have to tell Alex."

Nikos gaped at her. "Me?"

"You're his brother."

Nice of someone to remember that. Nikos scowled. "Where is he?" he asked at the very moment he remembered. "Is he still with Mari Lewis?" he asked, knowing what the answer would be.

Julietta nodded. She gave him the aunts' address.

He shook his head. "I'll leave a note at the house. I've got a plane to catch."

Julietta caught his hand. She looked up at him with eyes as big as the moon. "Don't let it be for him like it was for you, Nikos," she begged. "Please!"

Like it was for him? He didn't know what she was talking about.

"Go to him. Bring him to me!" Her nails were digging into his wrist.

"The old man—"

"I'm not your father, Nikos! And I'm not asking you for him! I'm asking for me. And for Alex. Please."

The doctor appeared just then, his competent, soothing professional smile in place. "Well, let's see if this little one is serious, Julietta," he said.

Julietta didn't even look at him. She only looked at Nikos. "Please."

So he went to Mari's aunts'.

He saw Mari down at the dock before he made it to the house. The minute he saw her, he felt better, as if he wasn't carrying the world on his shoulders anymore. Or if he was, at least he wasn't carrying it alone.

Mari was here. She would share it with him.

"Julietta?" she said now, her own flushed cheeks paling at his news.

"She wants Alex."

"Of course. I'll get him." She started to run toward the house. "We'll be right with you."

"I can't stay. I've got a plane to catch. I just came to tell you."

She turned. "To tell me?" she echoed. "And that's all?"

He didn't like the look on her face. It asked for things he didn't want to give. He shrugged irritably. "She's not *my* wife."

"Alex is *your* brother."

"Interesting how everybody's remembering that now," Nikos said bitterly.

"What?" Mari looked confused. And he didn't really have the right to say that to her. She'd always remembered. She'd tried to get him to care, to be involved earlier.

He jammed his hands into the pockets of his jeans. "Never mind," he muttered.

Just then the sound of running footsteps approached them. "Mari! Time for sup—" Alex stopped dead at the sight of his brother. "Nikos?"

"Hi, Alex."

The little boy looked from Mari to Nikos and back again, confusion and wariness in his face. Nikos didn't want to see it. He didn't want to see the flicker of hope there, either. It reminded him too forcibly of his own continually thwarted hopes as a child. But that was about his father, he reminded himself. Fathers were far more consequential than brothers—and half-brothers, at that.

But Alex's father was half a world away, and unlikely to be of much use even if he'd been there.

Damn it.

Nikos turned to the little boy. "Listen, Alex," he said quietly, "I came to get you. Your mother needs you. She had to go to the hospital."

"Hospital?" Alex looked at Mari.

"She's been having a few contractions," Mari said. "You know? Remember when she'd let you put your hand on her tummy to feel it get all hard and tight?"

Alex nodded. "How come she has to go to the hospital for that?"

"Well, if it starts happening regularly it might mean she's going to have the baby. It was sort of a surprise, having them now, so she wants you to come see her, just in case she has to stay and have the baby."

"Now?"

"Now," Mari said.

"What about supper?"

"Aunt Em can put our supper in some dishes and we can bring it along. We can eat back at your house after we see your mommy. We'll have a picnic."

Alex's eyes lit up. "Really?"

Mari smiled. "Yes. Run on up and tell Aunt Em we have to go."

Nikos listened to the whole exchange with awe. She seemed to know exactly what to say, the right note to strike. She didn't make Alex promises she couldn't—or wouldn't—keep. She didn't play down any fears he might have, but she offered him support, friendship.

"Where were you when *I* was growing up?" Nikos muttered.

"Too young to be any use at all," Mari said. She started toward the house after Alex. Nikos followed, curious still to see these aunts of hers.

When he'd met them, he had a good idea how Mari came to be the way she was. They were warm and welcoming, caring and kind. They told him what a handsome fellow he was, and how much Alex resembled him, and wasn't it funny that his name was Nikos.

"You know," Aunt Em confided, "Mari thought she was supposed to be nanny to a Nikos!" She smiled gleefully. "Imagine, being nanny to you."

"Imagine," Nikos echoed faintly. Mari pretended not

to hear. He could see that her cheeks were red, though, as she gathered up the containers as Aunt Bett filled them.

"We really need to be going," she said, herding Alex toward the door. "Say thank you, Alex."

"Thank you," he parroted. But then he turned and gave each of her aunts a big hug. "Thank you for the cookies 'n' for playin' cards 'n' for letting me go in your sailboat. C'n I come again?"

"Of course, darling," Aunt Em said.

"By all means. A born sailor like you should have lots of sailboat rides," Aunt Bett said, then slanted a glance at Nikos. "And bring your brother with you next time."

Mari bustled in, gave them each a kiss, then grabbed Alex's hand, and with the containers in the other arm, hurried out to the car.

Nikos started toward the Jag.

"I'll follow you," Mari said. "And don't expect me to keep up if you drive fast." She turned to Alex. "You'll make sure he drives slow enough for me, won't you?"

The little boy looked at her, speechless.

So did the big one. "Now wait a minute," Nikos began.

But Mari nailed him with a look. "I'm sure Alex would prefer a ride in a great car like yours to an old clunker like mine." She went around and opened the passenger door of the Jag. "Come on, Alex."

"Just a damn—"

"A-hem!"

Nikos scowled at her, but he shut his mouth.

The frost in her glare turned to a sweet smile. "It's

the best idea,'' she said lightly, but Nikos heard the underlying firmness in her voice.

''Fine,'' he muttered. ''See you there.''

The Jag had always seemed just right for two. When one of them was a pretty woman it almost seemed too big. When one of them was Alex, it wasn't nearly large enough. The child seemed to be sitting right on top of him!

Nikos drove fast, but not too fast, through the narrow back roads between the north and south forks of Long Island. Behind him he could see Mari's headlights in his rearview mirror.

Next to him, Alex sat unmoving, neck craned to see out the windshield. Only when the hospital came in sight did Nikos hear a sound out of him, and it wasn't a word so much as a tiny desperate gasp for air.

Instinctively Nikos reached over and put his large hand over one of Alex's small ones. Little fingers curled around his, tight. They hung on.

Nikos glanced down. Alex was still staring straight ahead, teeth biting down on his lower lip. Nikos pulled into a parking place and cut the engine, then gave Alex's hand a squeeze.

The boy turned his head and looked at Nikos with big worried eyes. ''I want my daddy,'' he whispered.

Nikos's throat tightened. His teeth clenched. He had consciously to ease the muscles in his jaw. ''I know,'' he said hoarsely. ''But your dad isn't here right now. Mari and I are, though. We'll come with you if you want.''

He didn't know why he was saying that! Well, yes, actually he did. He was saying it because they were words he'd needed to hear when he was a child when his own mother had been taken to the hospital and—

He couldn't remember. Until this moment he hadn't even remembered that his mother had gone to the hospital. Now he did. He remembered the long corridors. The odd metallic sounds. The hushed voices. He remembered sitting there alone, with people walking past him, talking around him, over him. Forgetting him.

It was as if he wasn't even there.

But he was. It was his father who hadn't been.

Just the way he wasn't here now. Nikos got out of the car and went around, taking Alex's hand in his. "Come on," he said. No one was going to do to Alex what they'd done to him.

Mari didn't know what had happened between Nikos and Alex on the trip from her aunts' to the hospital. All she knew was that, when she got out of her car in the lot and went to meet them, something had changed.

Nikos wasn't completely different. He wasn't embracing the whole notion of being involved with Stavros and his family, but something had happened. It was obvious in the way he stood next to Alex, almost protectively. She heard it in the firm voice with which he spoke to the hospital staff, and in the gentle reassurance with which he took the boy down the hall to see his mother.

This was the Nikos that Stavros had always wanted and feared didn't exist. This was a responsible, capable, caring man taking charge.

Mari didn't say a word. She just stood back and watched. She went with them down to see Julietta because Nikos's expression included her when he said, "We want to see Mrs. Costanides." She did talk to Julietta, calmly and optimistically, because in his stepmother's hospital room, Nikos didn't say much.

But he was there. He held Alex's hand while Mari talked to Julietta. He stood back next to Mari and waited while Alex went up to his mother's bed. Julietta touched her son's face and kissed him. She talked in a low, soft voice to him, explaining that the baby might be coming early and she had to wait here and see.

"Can I stay, too?" Alex wanted to know.

Julietta smiled. "There's only one bed in here. And Mari says she'll spend the night with you at home. That will be better than staying here. And then tomorrow we'll know if the baby is coming or not. If not, I can come home. Okay?"

Alex nibbled on his lip for a minute, then nodded. "I guess," he said, then looked back over his shoulder. "Is Nikos coming, too?"

Standing beside him, Mari could almost feel Nikos stiffen at the little boy's words. A fierce tension seemed almost to emanate from him. But it wasn't an angry tension. It was more like an intense very personal vibration. A sort of force field. Magnetic. Almost without realizing it, Mari drew closer.

Their arms brushed against each other. She felt Nikos's fingers grip hers. His hand was cold and damp, the clasp of his hand hard. She rubbed her thumb across his knuckle.

"Are you, Nikos?" Alex persisted.

"If you want me to." The words seemed dragged up from Nikos's toes.

Alex nodded solemnly. "I do."

It shouldn't have reminded Mari of a wedding. It was a four year old boy and his much older brother. But there was a sense of something sacramental about it. A vow. A promise.

She gave Nikos's hand a gentle squeeze and got a death grip in return.

"Nikos?" Julietta raised her voice, and Nikos's gaze jerked up to meet hers. His stepmother smiled mistily at him. "Thank you."

He was out of his flaming mind.

He shouldn't be here! *Couldn't* be here. Never in a million years would have believed he was here in his father's house, waiting while Alex put on his pajamas and got ready for bed.

But even as he thought it, he knew there was nowhere else he could possibly be.

And Mari knew it, too.

She watched him as carefully as she'd been watching Alex—as if she really was his nanny, concerned for his welfare above all else.

After they'd talked to Julietta, whom they left resting, Nikos had taken Alex back out to the car, while Mari stayed on a few minutes longer at Julietta's request, getting an earful of the things Alex didn't need to hear. But only a few minutes later she hurried to meet them by the car, cheerful smile in place as she said, "All set for that picnic, you two?"

Alex, who had been yawning and holding Nikos's hand silently, brightened at once and answered for both of them. "Yep. I'm starved."

Mari didn't even bother to warm the dinner, just served it cold to the three of them as they sat on a cloth spread on the deck overlooking the pool. Nikos looked at it doubtfully, but didn't say anything. Mari seemed to know what she was doing. And she proved it again because by serving it cold she got at least half a meal down Alex before he fell fast asleep on a chaise by the pool.

"You knew he was fading," Nikos said.

"There are signs. He's had a hard day. You have, too," she added. "How's your head? And your leg? I haven't even had time to ask."

Nikos shrugged. "They're all right." He picked up his jacket and put it over the sleeping boy.

"It was...kind of you to stay."

His mouth twisted wryly. "That's me, kind."

"Don't disparage yourself," Mari said sharply. "I know how hard it was for you."

No, you don't, he wanted to say. But, oddly, he felt as if she really did know. As if she had been there with him all day, feeling what he felt, sharing his pain, halving it. "Yeah," he said, his voice low. He stared out across the pool, a turquoise gem, glowing from its underwater light.

He didn't let himself look at her. If he did, he would see her mouth and remember her kisses. He would see her hair and remember its softness. He would see her body and remember its response.

His own was responding even now.

He shoved himself awkwardly to his feet and bent to pick up the sleeping child. "I'll carry Alex in. Get his bed ready, will you?"

Mari scrambled up as well and hurried into the house ahead of him. He gave her a good headstart. He stood there on the deck by the pool, the warm weight of his small brother in his arms, and tried to divorce himself from the moment.

Think about Cornwall, he told himself. *Think about Brian and Claudia, about Carruthers, about the life you want.*

But tonight he wanted something else. Something he couldn't have. Something he wouldn't let himself have.

And tomorrow? He prayed he wouldn't want it tomorrow.

And if he did?

He wouldn't let himself think about that.

"She wants me to *what?*"

"Don't shout. You'll wake Alex," Mari warned him.
They were in the living room of the main house. Nikos
had just put Alex in his bed and stood there looking
down at his little brother for a long moment. Then, res-
olutely, he'd turned away, heading back for the living
room, determined to get out now, before he did something he'd regret.

And now here Mari was, telling him to do the one
thing in the world he'd regret even more!

"Call Stavros? You're crazy!" He fumed. He paced.
He glared. "You don't mean it?"

"Julietta means it. She asked me to ask you."

"She didn't ask me herself!"

"Because she felt awkward."

"*This* is awkward!"

"I know that. But it has to be done. Someone has to
call him."

Nikos would have liked to have called his father every
name in the book! How the hell could the old man go
off and leave his wife when she was this close to having
his child?

"*You* call him," he suggested.

Mari shook her head. "I don't think anyone would
pay any attention to me. They'd pay attention to you."

"Pay attention to Nikos, his no-good playboy son?"
Nikos sneered.

"Maybe not. But they'd pay attention to Nikos, the
responsible man I saw take over at the hospital."

Nikos growled. He muttered. Mari didn't say anything else. He wished she would! It was easier to argue with someone than to argue with himself—especially when he was losing!

"He deserves not to be here," he snapped at her. "If he doesn't have the sense to stay when she needs him, he *deserves* to miss it."

"But does Julietta deserve not to have his support?"

Damn her! Damn her gentle logic! Damn her quiet confidence that he would come around and do the right thing!

He didn't *want* to do the right thing! He wanted Stavros to suffer.

But he didn't want Julietta to suffer. It wasn't her fault. And it wasn't Alex's fault. And the last thing Alex had murmured as Nikos had put him in bed was, "Night, Da…"

"Oh, hell! All right."

Nikos snatched the phone off the hook and stalked out of the room. He'd find the old man if he had to fly to Athens and knock down the Parthenon to get to him.

It just about came to that.

It was early morning in Athens and very late that night in New York when Nikos finally bullied his way through enough flunkies to get to Adrianos, one of his father's top aides.

"What's your business with him?" they all asked.

"None of yours," Nikos snapped over and over.

He wasn't telling any of them. No one but the old man. He didn't care if it took forever. The blistering he gave Adrianos brought his father, at last, to the phone.

Stavros was indignant. "Ah, Nikos, to what do I owe the pleasure of your phone call?" His tone was acidic. "Is the nanny being too hard on you?"

Nikos let his sarcasm pass. "Your wife's in the hospital," he said flatly. "Get your ass home."

There.

He'd done everything they'd asked of him. He'd taken Julietta to the hospital. He'd brought Alex to see her. He'd eaten a picnic with his brother. He'd put him to bed. He'd gritted his teeth and spent three hours tracking down his father. The old man was on his way home.

Nikos was out of here.

What more could anyone ask?

"What do you mean, I have to pick him up?" He stared at Mari, horrified. Furious. "I'm not going to get him! Let Thomas go get him."

"It's Thomas's day off," she reminded him gently.

"Then he can take a cab."

"He can't take a cab."

"He can afford it!"

"It's not a matter of affording it. It's that he needs someone to meet him."

"Not me!"

"He sounded shattered when he called from London. He—"

"He damned well ought to be!" Nikos was giving no quarter.

"I agree. But even he needs support," Mari went on firmly. "He needs his family there now." She looked at him. "You."

They glared at each other. Nikos raked his fingers through his hair. "*You* go get him then."

"I'm not family. And—" she forestalled his protest "—I need to stay with Alex. He didn't sleep well. He came to me in the middle of the night. He was tired from excitement after yesterday. Now he's tired from stress. He needs routine.''

Nikos opened his mouth to argue with that, then shut it again. He couldn't argue because he knew it was true. He jammed his hands in the pockets of his trousers and scowled out the window at the sea. He didn't *want* to go get his father! Not for anything—or anyone—on earth.

"Mari?" a small voice came from the hallway. Alex stood there with a stranglehold on his rabbit.

Mari smiled. "Ah, there you are! Good morning, Alex."

"Morning," he said, then his gaze went straight to Nikos. He smiled shyly. "Hi," he said softly.

Nikos raked his fingers through his hair. "Hi," he said to his brother, his voice ragged even though he managed to give Alex a smile. Then he let out a harsh breath and looked at Mari. "All right," he said. "You win."

CHAPTER EIGHT

THE man who got off the airplane that afternoon didn't even look like his father.

If the gray-faced old man making his way into the terminal hadn't said, "Nikos?" in a shocked tone, Nikos might have let him walk on by.

Stavros seemed to have aged twenty years in the space of the week since he'd left. And he was clearly astonished to see Nikos there waiting for him.

"Believe me, I wouldn't be here," Nikos said before his father could comment, "if there had been anybody else."

"Is she...?" Stavros couldn't even get the words out. He groped for something to hang onto, and Nikos, without thinking, caught his father's arm to support him.

"She's holding her own," he said gruffly. "The contractions have stopped. I called the hospital before I came this morning."

"Thank God." The faintest color reappeared in Stavros's complexion. He swallowed and a tremor seemed to run through him. But then he straightened and pulled himself together.

Nikos let go of his arm. "Come on. Let's get going."

The drive to East Hampton took two and a half hours. They made it in silence except for his father's questions about Alex right after they left JFK.

"How is he? Is he all right?"

Nikos's jaw tightened. He didn't take his eyes off the road, but he didn't feel as if he could see it at all. For a

139

long minute he couldn't answer. He couldn't get words past the thickening in his throat. At last he nodded, and when he could speak, he said harshly, "Mari has him. She's good at what she does."

The look Stavros gave him was a hard and assessing look.

Nikos didn't care. Let the old man think whatever he wanted. Let him *wonder* whatever he wanted. Nikos deliberately flexed his fingers on the steering wheel and drove on.

If Stavros had more questions, he didn't ask them. He did pull out a cellular phone once and call the hospital. His relief at being allowed to speak directly to Julietta was profound.

"Ah, *agape mou!* Julietta, my love, how do you feel?"

Nikos's teeth clenched. *Don't play the devoted husband in front of me, old man.* He didn't want to hear it! He didn't even really believe it.

But though he began by doubting his father's sincerity, once the niceties were dealt with, and Stavros would customarily have lapsed into his normal curt, businesslike manner, with Julietta he was not curt or businesslike at all. His tone was soft, his questions gentle. This loving man, this agonized husband was Stavros Costanides?

This was his father?

Nikos's hands strangled the steering wheel. He stepped down harder on the accelerator. His leg hurt from the continued demands of driving. He wanted to stretch it. Ease it. *Kick something.* Someone.

He thought he might explode.

They continued in silence. Nikos drove straight to the hospital. It wasn't until he'd pulled up out front and said,

"I'll take your gear to your place," that his father spoke again.

Stavros sighed just slightly and looked down at his hands before he turned his gaze to meet his son's. "Nikos," he said. His voice was as gentle as Nikos had ever heard it when speaking his name.

He looked away.

"Nikos," his father said again, and didn't move to get out until Nikos had looked back at him. "Thank you."

"I didn't want his damned thanks!" Nikos was prowling the length of the patio overlooking the pool where Mari was sitting and watching while Alex paddled in the shallow water. She'd seen Nikos coming and had sent her own prayer of thanks winging heavenward.

She'd had visions of him dropping Stavros off at the hospital, then taking straight off for London, figuring he'd done more than enough, and washing his hands of the whole mess.

But he was here. Limping. Irritable. Irascible. Annoyed. But *here*. And Mari breathed a sigh of relief.

"I know," she said softly now. "But keep your voice down or Alex will hear."

Nikos scowled, but he stopped fuming, and he stopped muttering. He stood, instead, just watching his brother play. There was a gentleness on his face, when he watched Alex, that Mari never saw there any other time.

"He's very like you," she said.

Nikos grunted. "More than you know."

She cocked her head to look at him, wanting him to continue, praying that he would.

"I've been where he is," was all he said.

"Nikos?" Alex stopped jumping in the water and looked up at his brother. "Can you come swimmin'?"

Nikos started to shake his head, to say no. Then he stopped. He glanced at his watch. "For a little while. I have a plane to catch."

"A plane?" Mari felt a sinking feeling in her stomach.

"Cornwall. Brian. My work. Remember?" Nikos said.

"Yes, but—"

"I'm not going to stay here. They don't need me!"

Mari thought they did, but she didn't think an argument would convince him. She just looked at him sadly.

Nikos didn't look at her at all. "How about going down to the ocean?" he said to Alex.

His little brother beamed. "Oh, yeah!" He started scrambling out of the pool.

Nikos took Alex down to the ocean. Mari didn't go with them. There were things that needed to be done here. And someone needed to stay around to take the calls if Stavros rang. Or Brian, for that matter, she thought glumly.

She glanced toward the beach. Nikos and Alex were standing on the shore, side by side. Nikos seemed to be talking, then Alex looked up and answered. Then they stood there again. Just as she was about to turn and go into the house, she saw Alex reach out and touch his brother's hand. She saw Nikos wrap his bigger hand around his brother's small one.

The two of them stepped closer together.

It was odd the way he felt bonded with Alex.

Or maybe it wasn't odd. The two of them shared a common parent. A pretty unfortunate tie, as far as Nikos could see. But no one else shared it. And as much as he personally would have liked to have washed his hands of his father, he couldn't quite do it yet.

Not until he'd told Alex what no one had ever told him.

It was easier somehow in the ocean. The ocean had always seemed to Nikos, ever since his childhood, to be his home. It was easier to understand than the people he'd lived with—his loving, doting, supportive mother, who let herself be hurt by a man not worthy of her love; his hard, unyielding father, who demanded so much and gave so little. Nikos loved the former, despised the latter—and understood neither.

It was easier to be by himself on the ocean. Sailing had been his salvation. Swimming had been his joy. Just sitting by the water had soothed him when the various sides of his world had seemed at odds with each other.

Until now he'd gone there alone. No—once at least he'd come close to bringing someone else. Mari—the day they'd gone to Montauk.

He'd barely known her then, but somehow he'd sensed that she would love it the way he did. Watching her drive his car had taught him that. It was the same feeling—being small and yet taking on something powerful, harnessing the power and making it your own.

He'd done it with the sea. Mari had done it with his Jaguar. Yesterday she'd taken Alex to sail, to share that love with him. Alex had told him about it while they'd walked down to the sea together.

"We sailed," he'd told Nikos. "Fast!" His eyes were bright. "Mari let me hold the rudder."

"Tiller," Nikos corrected gently.

"Yeah, that. We went soooo fast!" Alex had given a little hop. "I never been so fast. We're gonna do it again.

We're gonna go to her aunts' and go sailing again. Do you want to go, Nikos?'' He'd looked up at his brother, his eyes shining. "I wish you would go, Nikos."

And Nikos had smiled. "Yeah, Alex. I'd like that."

Alex's trust made it easier to tell him—to say the words he needed to say, that Alex, even if he didn't know it yet, needed to hear.

They were together, out in the ocean, far enough out so that Nikos was holding Alex in his arms while they bobbed up and down as the swells pushed toward the shore. "Alex, if you ever…need, um…if you ever need…anyone—" he couldn't say *me* "—if you ever need anyone…for anything…you can always call me. Always."

Alex, who had been bouncing against his chest, seemed to sense Nikos's sudden seriousness. He stopped and looked. Their eyes, on a level this once, locked. It was like looking into a mirror, Nikos thought.

For a long moment Alex didn't say anything, and Nikos wondered if he understood, or if he was too young…if what he remembered—the desolation, the loneliness, the anguish—were his alone. A projection, nothing more.

And then Alex bumped his forehead against Nikos's. "Good." And then he giggled and nipped Nikos's nose.

Mari met them coming up from the beach.

They were running, but Nikos was lagging a little behind, letting Alex take the lead. They were laughing. They looked like father and son. At least, Mari thought, they were acting like brothers.

And a good thing, too.

She hurried on, needing to reach them, to tell them.

"Mari! I catched a wave!" Alex yelled. "Me an' Nikos rode a wave!" He lunged forward and threw his small wet arms around her legs.

Mari caught him, hugged him close, but her eyes raised to meet Nikos's.

"What's up?" He arrived just as wet and a whole lot more desirable than his little brother. His dark eyes searched her face.

She mustered a smile. "Do you want the good news or the bad news first? The good news is they've got the labor stopped and Julietta is resting comfortably. The bad news is...your father had a heart attack."

CHAPTER NINE

ON SUNDAY, Julietta, worried but stable, came home.

Brian, worried, called almost hourly about Carruthers—who to Nikos's way of thinking was definitely *un*stable—and his latest revisions of the boat they were building for him.

Stavros, out of danger and stable for the moment, was still in the hospital where he was the doctors' problem. Nikos was glad. Anyway, there was nothing he could do for the old man.

"You'll be fine. Just fine," he told Mari firmly Sunday evening as they sat in the living room of the little cottage where they had brought Alex for the night so that Julietta could get some rest. "Everything's under control. And for you actually," he went on cheerfully, "things couldn't be better."

Mari looked at him doubtfully. "Oh, really?"

"Sure," he said, not looking at her. He *couldn't* look at her, hadn't been able to do more than glance at her since he'd thought he was home free only to be thrown back into her company again. It was too tempting. *She* was too tempting. And she needed somebody far better than him. "They *need* a nanny," he told her now. "And you're the best. You've proved it. You've saved their necks over the past few days."

"Not just me!" she exclaimed. "You—"

He cut her off. "You wondered what you were going to do when I left? Now you know. The old man will be eating out of your hand just for being here and taking

146

over. He'll give you whatever you want." It was true. All of it. The only bad part was, if she was working for his father, sometime, somehow, he would probably see her again.

"So it's perfect." He forged on. "And it's fine for me, too. I was here when you...when you needed me. And now I'd be in the way if I stayed. Besides, I can do my work better there."

He still didn't look at her. But he made the mistake of looking at Alex, playing cars on the floor, instead.

Alex looked up at him, dark eyes serious. "But *I* need you here, Nikos," he said.

It felt like they were playing house.

Like Mari was the mommy and Nikos was the daddy and Alex was the little boy. There was, of course, this underlying strain in Nikos that Mari couldn't pretend she didn't see. But at least she didn't think Alex saw it.

And Alex, of course, was the reason he stayed.

She knew it was for Alex, not for her. But she couldn't help herself—she was glad he was there. At some point she had quit lying to herself about it being the passion that was important. Certainly passion was important.

But Nikos was more important.

She loved him.

She wasn't sure when she stopped lying to herself about that, too. She thought it might have been when he went to get Stavros at the airport, even though she knew it was hard. She thought perhaps it was when she saw him with Alex on the shore, hand in hand. But she knew for sure when Alex looked up at him and said, "I need you here, Nikos," and he stayed.

She knew it was hard. She knew he hurt. She wanted to heal him.

She wasn't sure how.

She thought he was avoiding her, but it didn't seem like he was angry at her. More like she made him nervous.

She asked him why.

He looked at her like she'd grown antlers on her head. "Why the hell do you think?" They were sitting on the beach, watching Alex build a sandcastle. Or rather *Nikos* was watching Alex build a sandcastle. Mari was watching Nikos. She had been all day.

He'd looked at her once—just after breakfast. And, catching her eye, he'd looked abruptly away. He had studiously avoided looking her way ever since. He'd tried to discourage her from coming with him and Alex to the beach.

"It will give you a break," he'd said.

But Alex had wanted her to come. "She hasn't seen me body surf," he'd told Nikos.

"You're not missing much," Nikos had said under his breath so only Mari could hear.

But Alex had pleaded and Mari had wanted to go anyway, so she'd come.

But Nikos hadn't looked at her. Still.

"You act like you're mad at me. Like you don't want me here. Don't you?" she asked him bluntly.

He looked at her then, his dark eyes fathomless. "I want you in my bed." His jaw bunched tightly. His fist curled over a handful of sand.

Mari burned under the intensity of his gaze. And knew she wanted it, too. She swallowed. She ran her tongue over salty parched lips. "So do I," she said.

His eyes widened. He gave a hard quick shake of his head. "Don't say things like that."

"It's true."

"Even if it is, don't say things like that!" He shoved himself up and limped down the beach toward his brother.

Mari pulled her knees up to her chest and wrapped her arms around them. She watched him drop down on the sand next to Alex. She saw their two dark heads bent over the castle. Alex look her way, waved, beckoned her. Nikos said something to him, distracted his attention.

Oh, Nikos. I love you. Mari rested her head against her knees. *I would show you. I would sleep with you.*

But Nikos wouldn't sleep with her!

Did that mean he loved her, too?

He was a fool.

She'd virtually offered him her body. And he'd said no!

He needed to get out of here!

Regardless of what he'd promised Alex, he needed to leave. To get his own life back. At the very least, he needed to get out of here tonight. To stop playing house with Mari.

It would be fine if "playing house" extended to the bedroom. But he couldn't *let* it extend to the bedroom!

So he needed some other woman's bedroom. Some other woman's arms. Some other woman who could make him forget all about Mari Lewis's sweet face, her curvy body, her luscious mouth.

A man could be celibate just so long.

Nikos was way past that!

He waited until Julietta had retired to her room, until Alex had gone to bed, until there was just Mari and himself—and then he grabbed his jacket and headed for the door.

"Nikos?" She looked up from where she was sitting in the den. She had her shoes off and her feet tucked up under her. Her hair was loose, framing her face, making him focus on it—on her mouth.

"What?" he said harshly, still moving toward the door.

"Do you have work to do? Did Brian call? Do you want some help?"

"No. I don't need help. Or not that kind anyway! I need—" he glared at her "—damn it all, you *know* what I need!"

And he slammed out.

He could find it in East Hampton. He could go into a bar and meet some lonely woman, someone who wanted just one night and nothing more. There were plenty of women like that—refugees from the city, come out to the Hamptons for a little R&R.

It wouldn't be a problem. No problem at all.

He'd have his pick, he was sure.

The trouble was, he discovered, after four bars and four times that many likely women, he found something wrong with all of them. This one was too forward, that one was too tall. This one was a redhead. That one was blonde.

None of them had a sunny smile and an infectious giggle. None of them had lips begging to be kissed. At least not by him.

They'd have been willing—if he had.

He couldn't do it.

Damn it to hell!

What was the matter with him?

Maybe he needed a celebrity. Maybe all his days as

a globe-trotting playboy had spoiled him. Maybe he needed a photographer and notoriety to spark his interest.

But in the fifth bar he found a model he'd dated once or twice, one he'd been photographed with on several occasions. Where Karla went, photographers went—so if that was his problem, Karla could fix it.

And Karla was clearly willing.

But Nikos said, "I can't," when she asked him back to the house she was renting for the week.

"Can't?" Karla looked at him, astonished. He doubted very many men said no.

"I...have to get back," he said. "My brother..." *Oh, good,* he berated himself, *start dragging Alex up as an excuse.* "I can't," he said again.

Karla's brows lifted. "Brother?"

Nikos shook his head. He wasn't going into that. "I'll...see you around."

"Of course, darling," Karla said. She pursed her lips for a kiss.

Nikos ducked in, but turned his head at the last moment. His lips grazed her cheek.

She looked at him, eyes as big as soup bowls. But Nikos couldn't explain. He didn't understand himself. He just knew he had to get out of there.

He got into the Jaguar and drove. And drove.

He drove for hours, it seemed—along one back road after another. From one side of the island to the other. At two in the morning he found himself sitting in the Jag overlooking the dock by Mari's aunts' house.

Damn, he thought. *Oh, hell.*

Damn, she thought. *Oh, hell.*

She thought a few other unprintable things over the

next few hours. She couldn't decide if she was more furious or more hurt.

She knew, of course, what he was doing. He was out bedding another woman. Having sex with another woman. She refused to say *making love* with another woman. She was sure that love had nothing to do with it—unless it was because he was running scared from his love of her.

Did he love her?

Or was that merely wishful thinking? Had she gone beyond Mary Poppins, right into a Pollyanna approach to life?

Mari sat in the dark on the deck and tried to sort things out. It wasn't easy. For a long time after Julietta's light had gone out and Alex had long since gone to sleep, she'd paced the house and the grounds.

How dare Nikos just up and leave like that? How dare he imply that it was somehow her fault?

She hadn't refused him, for heaven's sake! In fact— and she blushed as she recalled it—this afternoon she had frankly admitted she wanted to go to bed with him, too!

But had he taken her up on it?

No. He'd acted like she'd said something wrong! Like she was Eve, holding out the apple that would damn him!

Mari would like to damn him right now.

She jumped to her feet and began to prowl again, turning every once in a while to glare down the drive toward the road in the direction he'd gone. Where was he? Who was he with?

It didn't bear thinking about!

She should have gone to sleep hours ago. She couldn't. She'd tried about midnight. She'd put on a pair of sleep shorts and a T-shirt, and she'd gone to bed. But she couldn't sleep. She'd tossed and turned and thought of Nikos.

Nikos the traitor.

Nikos. In bed with another woman.

There had been no use staying in bed trying to sleep when thoughts like that played havoc with her mind. She got back up. She went outside. She went up to the big house and checked on Julietta and on Alex. All was well.

She went back outside.

The night was still and almost moonless. There was no light but that since she'd shut off the pool light hours ago. There was no wind either—except the searing awful wind of pain that blew through her when she thought about Nikos with someone else. She needed to do something—to work off the feelings that buffeted her.

A sail would have been wonderful. But it was the middle of the night and she had no boat.

A swim, then. The ocean always helped. If she couldn't be on it, she could be *in* it. But she knew better than to do that, too. She wouldn't swim alone in the ocean. Not when no one knew where she had gone.

But she could swim in the pool.

And so she did. She shed her shorts and shirt and dove straight in. Who was there to see, after all?

Nikos?

Hardly. And if he were there, he would turn his back!

She swam long and hard. Lap after lap. Back and forth. On and on. As if swimming would purge her need, cleanse her soul, calm her emotions.

It tired her out. Her heart beat from the exertion. Her pulses raced from the effort expended. But the need was still there when she finally glided to the deep end, crossed her arms on the tiles and rested her chin on them.

The need was still there. Not even dulled. Sharper, if anything, because it was the strongest feeling in her. Passion.

Once she'd marvelled at it, had been amazed to feel it. Now it was her constant companion. Since she'd met Nikos, it wouldn't leave her alone.

He would, though. He had.

He was with someone else.

Slowly Mari hauled herself out of the water. She stood naked on the tiles, dripping, letting the night air dry her. She wrung the water out of her hair and combed it back with her fingers.

And then headlights came around the curve of the long drive and caught her full force. She stopped, frozen.

The car stopped, too. Jerked to a halt with an instant's screech of the brakes.

Then Mari reached for her clothes, snatched them up and tried to pull them on, hopping toward the house as she did so. *Damn! Oh, damn!*

And then Nikos was out of the car, limping towards her as fast as he could.

She almost made it into the house. She had her shorts on, had the T-shirt almost over her head. And he caught up with her, turned her in his arms, and lowered his mouth to hers.

She should have fought him. He hadn't wanted her! He'd turned his back on her, gone to someone else!

She tried to fight him. But he held her fast, wrapped his arms around her, pressed her wet body to his.

"God, Mari! What you do to me!" He gasped the words against her mouth. He ground his body against hers, showing her all too clearly that, whoever he'd been with, his desire for her had not slackened.

She pushed at him. "Go away! You don't want me! You wanted—''

"I want you! How could you think I don't! You're killing me.''

"You left!''

"Because I *shouldn't* want you!''

Their bodies were tangling as they spoke. He kissed her mouth, her cheeks, her eyes. He threaded his fingers through her hair, tugging lightly, tipping her head back to give him greater access. He kissed her neck, her jaw, her ears.

"You went to someone else!''

"I didn't.''

"Don't lie.''

"I'm not lying. I wanted to. I needed to! I couldn't.'' He sounded disgusted with himself.

Mari pushed him back and tried to see his expression. It was too dark. She could only hear his labored breathing, feel the hardness of his body, the grip of his fingers on her arms. "Is that true?'' she asked quietly.

She heard him swallow. She felt the shudder that ran through him when he exhaled sharply. "It's true.''

"You were going to.'' It wasn't a question.

"Yes. Of course I was. You want forever. I'm not offering forever. So how could I use you?''

"Use?''

"That's what it would be,'' he said harshly.

"No.'' She didn't believe that. No matter what he thought he was doing, she was sure he wasn't capable of using her. And she wouldn't be using him. Once she might have—not to make love with, but to learn about her capacity for passion. But this had only peripherally to do with passion. It had only to do with him.

"What do you mean, no?'' Nikos rasped.

"I love you," she told him.

He stopped dead. Didn't speak. Didn't move. Didn't even seem to breathe. Then, "No, you don't," he said.

She touched his lips. "I do." She remembered Alex saying those same words and her thinking it sounded like a wedding promise. It sounded like a vow when she said it now, too.

Nikos must have thought so, too, for he pulled abruptly away. He turned his back. He bent his head and hunched his shoulders as if weighed down by some great burden. Then he tipped his head back and threw back his shoulders and stared at the sky as if the answers were there.

The answers, Mari could have told him, weren't anywhere out there. They were inside him.

"I'm not promising forever," he said finally, turning his head toward her. His voice was rough—with need and tension and, perhaps, something else. There was no harshness, though. It was as if he was warning her.

Mari understood.

She reached out a hand and touched his arm. A tremor went through him. She ran her hand down his arm to touch his fingers. She wrapped her own around them. For a long moment he didn't move, as if he was giving her one last chance to back out.

But Mari wasn't backing out.

She was going to love Nikos Costanides—and she was going in head—and heart—first.

He'd thought she was a mirage. An illusion.

He'd thought that one whiskey he'd downed had gone straight to his brain, making him see things that weren't there.

That wasn't really Mari Lewis *naked* on the poolside, was it?

He'd slammed on the brakes, staring in disbelief until he saw her move. She'd reached for her clothes, grabbed them, and started toward the house.

And he knew he wasn't going to let her get that far.

He hadn't. He'd caught her. He'd kissed her. He'd allowed her to feel the feverish need he had for her.

He had wanted her desperately. He *still* wanted her.

He didn't want her to love him.

Why in God's name had she said that she loved him? *"Don't,"* he'd begged her. *"How could I use you?"* he'd asked her. *I'm not promising forever,* he'd warned.

But it hadn't done any good.

She'd taken his hand. She'd touched his face. She'd put her arms around him and let him feel the beat of her heart.

He couldn't say no any longer. A man could only take just so much.

He took Mari to the cottage, to his room. To his bed.

She went willingly, eagerly even. She sat on the bed and watched while he fumbled to get out of his clothes. His hands were shaking, and finally, with a small smile, she'd said, "Let me. I'm good at this."

For a second he scowled, thinking she meant she'd undressed a lot of men. But then he realized she was talking about undoing buttons and zippers. She was a nanny. It was her stock-in-trade.

She was the sexiest nanny he'd ever seen. The sexiest *woman*. It was all he could do to stand still and let her undo the buttons of his shirt and slide it off, ease down the zipper of his trousers and skim them down his legs. She dropped to her knees to do it. Her wet hair brushed against him. Through his shorts he could feel her. His teeth came together. His shut his eyes. His fingers curled into fists.

He stepped out of the shorts, reached for her, pulled her up against him, and fell back, carrying her with him onto the bed.

God, it felt good, having her body covering his like this. He'd dreamed about Mari Lewis in his bed since the first day he'd seen her. He'd tried not to think of her except as fully-clothed and poring over computer screens full of tankage volumes or playing with Alex on the floor. And during the daylight hours he hadn't done too badly.

The nights his unconscious had taken over, weaving fantasies that drove him wild. One of them had them lying together, Mari on top of him, her weight warm and wonderful, a prelude to her body taking him in.

This Mari was cool, her skin still fresh from her swim in the night air. But the longer she lay atop him, the warmer they became. The heat grew between them—the heat of desire, of need.

Of love, he knew Mari would say.

He couldn't say it. He could feel it, though. He slid his hands down her back, caught his thumbs beneath the elastic of her shorts and tugged them off. Her skin was so smooth, so slick, so soft. So cool. So warm. So hot.

He couldn't get enough of her.

And Mari's touch, as eager and frantic as his, said she felt the same way about him.

Of course she did. She loved him.

He didn't let himself think about that. It was a burden he couldn't carry. It was a promise he couldn't make.

"It's all right," she whispered, as if she knew. And he supposed she might because he had stopped just then.

His hands had ceased their stroking. His body had tensed, holding back.

"It's all right."

It wasn't. But he couldn't help it. He needed her now. He'd warned her. She knew what she was getting. All he could give. Not what she wanted, but what he was capable of.

"Come to me, Nikos." She beckoned. She rolled off him and drew him down upon her. Her hands played down the length of his spine, making him arch against her as they reached his buttocks. They stripped off his own shorts.

He made a sound deep in his throat. A hungry sound. A needy sound. He needed *her,* and it was with great anticipation that he settled between her legs, both of them naked at last.

He wanted to make it good for her. If he couldn't give her forever, he could at least give her the joy of the moment. And so he set about doing just that. But it wasn't only joy for her. He, too, was caught up in what was happening between them.

And when she drew him into her, even though he felt her body's resistance, he could not stop.

"It's all right," she said again because, he understood, she did not want him to stop. She wanted him—all of him. She gave him all of herself.

What was this intimacy they were sharing? How was it different than any other coupling he had ever shared?

Because it was. He knew that from the moment he was inside her.

It was touch. There was always touch. It was friction. But there was always that, too. It was fire, burning hot and strong and vital. But it was also something more.

Intimacy with Mari gave him something he'd never

come close to experiencing with any other woman. He couldn't describe it. Had no words.

Passion? Yes, but...

Desire? Of course, and...

Love?

That, he was sure, was what Mari was calling it. Maybe...maybe it was. He didn't know. Didn't care. It overcame him before he could define it. It drew him in, encircled him, tied him down...

And freed him at the same time.

And when he felt her body shiver around his, when he felt her pulse with release and heard her gasp, "Oh!" as if she'd never experienced anything like this, he knew exactly how she felt.

He felt the same way.

Lost. And suddenly—in her embrace—found.

The phone woke them.

Nikos rolled away from Mari long enough to squint at the bedside clock before answering it. Almost four. He supposed he should be glad that Brian had given them a little more time.

"Whowizit?" Mari mumbled. She rolled with him, keeping him in her embrace. "Brian? C'rruthers?"

"Who else?" Nikos muttered. He didn't want to wake up. Didn't want the real world intruding on what he and Mari had shared. They'd had too little time as it was. He wanted more. Not much. A few hours. He wanted to love her just one more time.

"Can't you give me one night's peace?" he barked into the phone.

There was a long pause.

Then Julietta's wavering voice said, "Nikos? Is Mari with you? I...looked for her. I don't want to bother you. I'm sorry, but I think this is it. This time I really am in labor."

Like Julietta the thought was eased. "Mari," It hurt even more! "...to see for her. I couldn't let you bother you. I'm sorry. Not bother this now. This hurts. I really need to know."

CHAPTER TEN

THERE was no time to be embarrassed.

Mari had to throw on one of Nikos's long-tailed shirts and hurry to the house. There, in the bedroom she'd been using since Julietta had gone to the hospital the first time, she hurriedly dressed and then, despairing of getting a comb through her damp, hopelessly tangled hair, she loped down the hall to find Julietta huddled in her bed.

"They're four minutes apart and they're strong." Julietta's eyes were wide with dark smudges beneath. There was a waver in her voice, too, but it was stronger than it had been at the hospital before. And she didn't look panicky, just nervous. "The doctor said the more time, the better. I hope this is enough."

"It's enough," Mari said, and prayed that she was right.

Moments later Nikos came in. He wore clean jeans and an open-necked blue shirt, which wasn't entirely tucked in. Still, he looked far more put together than Mari knew she did. Having one's hair combed was indeed a help.

"Ready?" he asked Julietta.

She nodded toward the small suitcase by the dresser. "All packed. I just...need to go in and see Alex."

"You're going to wake him?" Nikos frowned.

Julietta shook her head. "Just see him." Holding her abdomen, she trundled into Alex's room and bent over him for just a moment. Her hand touched his hair and

162

he stirred slightly, but didn't wake. Then awkwardly she leaned down and dropped a kiss on his cheek. She looked at Mari, standing in the door to the hallway. ''All set now.''

Mari stepped out of the way. Nikos, who had put her case in the car, was just coming back in. He looked at Mari, his face whisker-shadowed and haggard, a hint of desperation in his eyes. Mari thought she knew what the desperation was about. He'd just realized that one of them was going to have to go to the hospital with Julietta. One of them might even have to coach her through her labor and delivery. One of them was going to have to tell Stavros. And one of them was going to get to stay home with Alex.

She knew what he expected her to say. She was, after all, the logical one to stay home. She was the nanny.

But she was *his* nanny. And in this case there was no deliberation at all. She had to do what was best for her charge. And in this case it was letting him stay with Alex. It was, if the truth were known, best for Alex, too.

They were brothers. They needed each other.

Later, when Alex was awake, when he could be a buffer between Nikos and the pain, that would be soon enough for them to come to the hospital.

She held out a hand to him. His was cold and clammy. She gave it a squeeze. ''You stay,'' she said. ''I'll go.''

Something flickered in his eyes. Something relaxed in his body. His fingers returned the squeeze and he nodded. ''We'll come later.''

Julietta looked at the two of them and smiled right before another contraction hit. Then she said, ''We'd better be going.''

''A girl?'' Alex looked doubtful when Nikos gave him the news several hours later. Julietta's labor had been quick. The baby was small, but apparently strong.

"Mother and daughter are doing well," Mari had called and told him a while ago. "You have a sister."

A sister. A dainty dark-haired child who would grow up to knock men's socks off, Nikos had no doubt. He supposed that meant he would have to be vigilant, protecting her from rakes and scoundrels. From men like him.

Men who took and didn't give.

But, some voice inside him argued, he hadn't taken from Mari last night. She had given—and he had received. It was the most beautiful gift he'd ever had. That was certain. He would cherish it the rest of his life.

He would cherish her.

But he wouldn't marry her. He didn't dare.

"Girls aren't bad," he said now, his voice a little rough. And at Alex's still dubious look, he ruffled the boy's hair. "You'll see."

Alex hopped around the kitchen, having finished the bowl of cereal Nikos had given him. "When? Can we go soon?"

"Soon," Nikos promised. "Just let me clean up here."

In fact it took a little longer than he thought. He had two phone calls, one from Claudia about regular business matters and another more desperate one from Brian a little later. He took some notes and promised to get right on it.

"Do that," Brian said. "And when the hell are you coming back? You're out of the cast now, aren't you?"

"Yeah. It's just...I've been needed here."

"Well, you're needed here, too, old man. I thought you weren't going to let your father run you."

"He's not. It has nothing to do with him."

"Whatever you say," Brian said. But Nikos didn't need much imagination to hear the skepticism in his voice.

He hung up rather more forcefully than necessary, then turned to Alex. "Come on. Let's go to the hospital."

She was a dainty dark-haired child. Just over five pounds, with a red mottled face and the longest eyelashes he'd ever seen.

"She looks sort of like a monkey," Alex whispered to him nervously, out of Julietta's hearing.

She did, in fact. But, "She'll grow out of it," Nikos assured him.

"Did I look like a monkey?" Alex asked.

"I didn't see you when you were a baby," Nikos admitted.

"How come?"

"I was...out of the country." And wouldn't have been willing to come and see this new half-brother even if he hadn't been. Though of course he didn't tell Alex that.

He'd considered Alex's birth more of his father's folly. It wasn't enough that he marry a trophy wife young enough to be his daughter! Then the old man had to go and get her with child. Nikos had been furious when he'd found out.

Now he didn't know what he felt.

Not fury certainly. Somewhere over the course of his stay in the cottage he'd seen real affection between his father and Julietta. As hard as it was to fathom, they actually acted like they loved each other. If he hadn't believed it before, he certainly did after seeing Stavros's white face when he got off the plane that afternoon and then overhearing his father's conversation with his wife.

That was no man talking to a trophy. That was a man in love.

But if seeing that his father really cared for Julietta had reconciled Nikos to his father's second marriage, it hadn't stopped the hurt.

What about his own mother? If Stavros actually had the capacity to love, why hadn't he loved *her?*

Of course Nikos wouldn't ask.

He hadn't seen his father since right after the old man's heart attack. Seeing Stavros with tubes and bags and monitors all around him had made Nikos ill. He'd felt himself get light-headed and, though assured by the nurse that his father was holding his own, Nikos couldn't stay.

"Better if I don't," he'd told Mari when she asked the next day if he was coming to the hospital with them. "Give him another one just to see me there."

She hadn't argued with him, which pretty much proved she felt the same way. She came back later and told him that things were looking good.

"He's stable. It was a mild attack, and his being in the hospital when it happened helped a lot."

Every day he'd improved—or so Nikos heard. He never went back.

Today, of course, he did. When Mari called and said the baby had been born, that Georgiana Elizabeth Costanides was alive and well and snuggled in her mother's arms, he'd known great relief. He'd been glad to take Alex, to stand outside the nursery and hold the little boy up so they could both look at the child in the pink blanket-lined bassinette.

"What do you think of your sister?"

The quiet, raspy Greek-accented voice behind Nikos almost caused him to drop Alex. He turned, holding the boy like a shield.

"Papa!" Alex crowed, and wriggled to get down, to run and embrace the man who leaned on a walker and looked at them both.

Reluctantly, slowly, Nikos let him down, then watched as the boy skirted the walker, then slowed down and carefully put his arms around his father's legs. One of Stavros's hands left the walker to touch Alex's hair, to stroke its softness. His gaze dropped, too. And then he raised it again.

"Nikos?"

There was something hard and huge in Nikos's throat. It took him a moment to get the word past it, but finally he managed. "Congratulations."

And then he turned away.

Mari found him at the far end of the parking lot.

He was standing with his back to the hospital, staring off into space, but she doubted if he was seeing anything.

She had witnessed the encounter between him and his father from the end of the hall. She'd seen the emotions as they had flickered across his face one by one. Surprise. Hurt. Need. Resignation. And then she'd seen him turn and walk away.

She'd wanted to run after him then. But she'd had to wait to be sure that Stavros could manage Alex. And by the time she'd finally got father and younger son settled in and visiting in Julietta's room, Nikos was long gone.

"Sit down," Stavros had commanded her when she moved restlessly about.

But Mari couldn't. She prowled the hallway, went to the waiting room, then came back. Even then she couldn't settle. In desperation she looked out the window—and that's when she saw him.

"I've got to go," she said. And, not caring what any of them thought, she hurried out.

"Mari?" she heard Julietta's concerned voice follow her.

"Miss Lewis!" Stavros's peremptory tone clearly expected her to stop.

But Mari didn't stop. Not until she was within ten feet of Nikos, facing his back. Then she did. She stopped, panicked.

It was practically the first time she'd spoken to him since they'd made love. They'd shared a few necessary sentences since—but none had to do with what had happened between them.

Now didn't seem exactly like the time to talk, either. But maybe it was time for something other than talk. Sometimes, she told the parents she worked with, talk didn't say what needed to be said.

Now, Mari suspected, was one of those times.

So, gearing up her courage, unsure what kind of a reception she was going to get, she came up behind him. "Nikos?"

He stiffened, then turned slowly, his eyes meeting hers. It was all still there—the hurt, the confusion, the pain, the resignation. But, for just an instant, she saw something else—something more. Something, she dared think, for her.

She opened her arms and stepped forward, sliding them around him, pressing against him. She didn't kiss him. She only held him. *I love you,* she told him silently—with her arms and her body and her warmth. This wasn't the passion she'd found with Nikos from the first moment. This was something deeper and something far more precious.

It was love.

She felt a tremor run through him. He stood stone-still. A statue. Not even breathing. And then she felt the weight as he laid his head against her hair. His arms came around her, too. His hands locked against her back, holding them together. He drew a long shuddering breath. First one, then another.

"I love you." She said the words now. She pulled back just a little, enough to look up into his eyes. "I love you," she repeated.

His gaze dropped for a moment, then lifted to meet hers again. "I know," he said, his voice ragged. "I know you do."

He made a reservation for London that afternoon. He would leave the following morning. He told Mari what he'd done that afternoon when she brought Alex home for dinner.

"You're leaving?" She stared at him in disbelief.

He hardened his heart against it. It was better this way, he assured himself. Yes, she loved him. But that didn't matter. When had love ever brought anything but pain? Look what it had done to his mother, after all.

He didn't want to hurt her the way his father had hurt his mother. He was sparing Mari pain.

If he was honest, of course, he had to admit he was sparing himself pain, too.

"I need to get back," he said implacably, ignoring the expression on her face. "I have a life there. A job. It's where I belong. I only stayed because of Alex. You know that. But Alex will be all right now. The baby's here. Julietta's fine. In a few days even Stavros will be home. No one will need me.'' He was glad Alex was playing in the other room. At least this time his little brother couldn't contradict him.

And Mari wouldn't. He knew that.

He knew, despite the pain he saw in her eyes, that she would let him go. It was the right thing for both of them. She could do far better than him. Ultimately she would understand that.

And he?

He would be fine. *He would be fine.* He would say it until it came true.

"I'm going in the morning," he told her. "I have to go."

He wouldn't do it. She didn't believe him.

He *couldn't* walk away from her so easily, she told herself. He couldn't just turn his back. He loved her, too! She knew he did.

But she couldn't insist. It was for him to say the words. They would mean nothing if she had to drag them out of him.

Say it, she begged silently. *Say you love me.*

But he didn't say anything at all.

He would see reason, Mari told herself. She pasted on as cheerful a smile as she could manage and, after supper, took Alex back to the hospital to see his parents and his new baby sister. They brought helium balloons, one for each, and Alex carried them proudly to each room.

They took Georgiana's to the nursery first. While Alex watched, the nurse tied the pink and silver foil bobbing heart to her bassinette.

"So she can see it when she looks up," Alex explained to Mari. He studied his sister through the glass.

"She is looking better," he decided. "The first time I saw her, she looked pretty much like a monkey."

Mari hid a smile. "She'll get better," she promised.

Alex nodded sagely. "That's what Nikos says."

Mari couldn't count the number of times over the last few days that Alex had quoted his brother. Nikos was clearly a hero in the little boy's eyes. Alex would miss Nikos. He couldn't leave Alex, could he?

They took Julietta her balloon next. Alex's mother was very much herself now that she'd had some rest and was past the stress of labor. She looked much more relaxed today. And she was thrilled with the balloon Alex gave her, tying it to the rail at the foot of her bed, saying, "So I can see it all the time."

"Just like Georgie," he said happily, hopping from one foot to the other. "Mari 'n' me brought Georgie one, too. An' this one's for my daddy." He jiggled the one with the happy face on it.

"Wonderful," Julietta said. "He'll be so happy to get it. Georgiana and I are going to get to come home tomorrow, and Daddy's going to have to stay here all alone."

"How come?" Alex asked.

"Because he needs a few more days' rest," Julietta told him.

Alex's lower lip jutted out. "But he's okay?" he insisted.

Julietta patted the bed and Alex scrambled up next to her, snuggling in. "He's okay, darling. He'll be fine." She gave him a quick hug. The bedside phone rang and she picked it up. Her eyes lit up.

"He's right here," she said. "Yes. Good idea. Are you sure you can walk that far? All right then." She hung up. "That was Daddy," she told Alex. "He's coming to visit, and he wants to know if you'll meet him by the nursery. You can take him his balloon.''

Alex beamed and hopped off the bed, running to the door.

''Walk,'' his mother called after him.

He slowed, but not much.

Julietta smiled. ''He's going to keep things lively,'' she said, shaking her head. ''I wish you were going to be staying to help me with him.''

Mari felt as if the bottom had dropped out of her stomach. ''I'm not?'' She shouldn't have said the words. They weren't professional. If Julietta didn't want her, she had no right to question it.

Julietta's brow furrowed. ''Well, I assumed you'd be going with Nikos when he goes…wherever he goes. We saw you two,'' she added, with a tip of her head toward the window, ''when you were in the parking lot. We thought…''

Yes, Mari had thought, too. Or maybe *hoped* was the truer word.

Now she shook her head. ''No. Nikos is leaving. Tomorrow morning.''

''What!''

Mari shrugged. ''He has to go.''

''You love him.'' Julietta had no doubt about that. Of course, she'd seen them together and, during the last few days of her pregnancy, she'd had nothing to do but watch—and think.

Mari knew there was no point in denying it. ''He's still leaving,'' she said.

''He loves you, too.''

She wouldn't argue that, either, though she suspected Nikos might. ''I don't think he wants to love anyone.'' She looked at Julietta, tried to smile, to sound brave and

determined, but there was such compassion and com-
miseration in Julietta's eyes that Mari couldn't look for
long. Her gaze slid away.

"Oh, Nikos," Julietta murmured sadly. She shook her
head and looked at Mari again. "Oh, my dear."

A smart woman in possession of the common sense God
gave her would not have spent the night in Nikos
Costanides's bed.

Mari was a smart woman with a lot of common sense.
She didn't go to Nikos. But she couldn't say no when
he came to her.

Alex had fallen asleep on the way home from the
hospital. He'd bounced out to the car, chattering ani-
matedly about how much his daddy liked the balloon
and how good it was going to be to have his mother and
Georgie home tomorrow.

"An' pretty soon my daddy, too," he'd said happily.
"And then we'll all be together."

And the next thing she knew he was sound asleep in
the seat. She parked close to the house and was carrying
him up the walk when Nikos opened the door.

Wordlessly he came and lifted Alex from her arms.
He carried the little boy with the ease of a father as he
strode along the hallway to his brother's bedroom and
put Alex into his bed.

Mari took the child's shoes off, then covered him with
the duvet, leaving his shorts and T-shirt on. If he woke
later she could get him into pajamas, but she didn't think
he would. It had been a busy day. He was tired. She bent
and kissed him, then stepped back.

Nikos dropped down to his knees by the bed and
looked at his little brother. One hand came out and
smoothed Alex's hair. A knuckle brushed his petal-soft

cheek. Then Nikos, too, pressed a light kiss on his forehead, and got up and followed Mari out of the room.

It was his goodbye to his brother, and she knew it.

If she'd had any hope that he would stay, she lost it then. If he couldn't face Alex and tell him he was leaving, if he couldn't look his brother in the eye and say goodbye, then she knew he was really and truly going.

Maybe that was why she let him come to her that night. So she'd have one more memory to drag out in a lifetime of regret. She hadn't had long with Nikos Costanides. She needed all the memories she could get.

She dared to hope that he needed them, too. His desperation as they made love told her without his having to say anything that he did. If their first night's loving had been strong and urgent and powerful, it was nothing compared to this one.

It was all those things—and gentle besides. His touches were tender, his kisses urgent. His hands made her whimper and reach for him and writhe. She did her share of loving him, too. She had a lifetime of love to teach him in just one night. She molded his face with her hands, memorizing the strong cheekbones, the firm line of his jaw, the sharpness of his nose. She studied his lips, traced them with her fingertip and then her tongue. She kissed his lashes, ran her fingers through his hair, kissed his chest, his navel, let her mouth dip below.

He sucked in a ragged breath and dragged her up the length of his body. "Enough," he muttered as he fitted them together.

But though they loved all night, Mari never got enough.

She didn't think Nikos did, either. His hands were still stroking her, petting her, holding her, as his body spooned around her and they slept.

*   *   *

She was asleep when he left.

It was all right not to wake her and say goodbye. They'd said goodbye all night long. They'd loved…and loved…and loved. Words couldn't have said anything more.

It was better this way.

Better this way. The words echoed in his mind, a mantra that he said over and over, all the way to the airport. He was doing what he wanted to do. What he needed to do. What was better for her—and for him. He was doing the right thing.

Still, once he got to the airport, he wanted to get on his way! He didn't understand why they had to make him be there two hours before the international flight. Once he was there, he was ready to go. If he was leaving, he wanted to be gone, damn it, gone.

He paced the terminal, scowled out the window, slumped in a chair, then got back up, irritated, distracted, and stared out the window some more.

"Nikos?" The voice was low, raspy, familiar, Greek. Totally out of place.

He spun around.

His father stood right behind him, leaning on a cane, breathing in short shallow breaths, his forehead damp from exertion, his face pale.

"What the hell—?" Nikos shook his head. "What are you doing here? You're supposed to be in the hospital!"

"I checked myself out."

"Why? Do you have a death wish, for God's sake!" Nikos grabbed his father's arm and towed him to a chair and sat him down. He didn't sit down beside him. He stood, glowering, his own heart beating double time.

"Sit," Stavros commanded. He patted the chair next to him.

"I don't want to sit. I'm going to be sitting for six hours!"

Stavros looked up, straight into Nikos's eyes. "Sit."

A muscle ticked in Nikos's temple. He ground his teeth. He rocked back on his heels. He glared at his father. He sat.

"Good." Stavros nodded and took a slow breath. "I come to tell you a story."

"A story?" Nikos was incredulous. "You checked yourself out of the hospital and drove two and a half hours to tell me a story?"

"Thomas drove," Stavros admitted. "I tell you a story."

"So tell me, damn it! Then go home and get back to bed. You're going to die if you don't! You don't want to die. You've got little kids to take care of."

"You would take care of them," Stavros said confidently. He looked at Nikos, his expression almost serene.

Nikos's jaw worked. "You're so sure of that, are you?"

"I am." A faint smile touched Stavros's face. "I saw you with Alex."

Nikos looked away. "He's a good kid," he muttered.

"He is like his brother was."

"*Was* being the operative word."

"Is," Stavros corrected himself.

Nikos looked at him sharply. "Revising your opinion, are you?"

"Yes." There was no apology. Just a statement of fact. He wouldn't have been Stavros, of course, if he had said he was sorry. Still, Nikos felt a small stab of satisfaction.

"I tell you the story," Stavros said. He looked straight ahead out the window, watching planes on the runway while he spoke. "It is about a young man with big ideas. It is about a woman he fell in love with. It is about me—and your mother."

Nikos stared. He didn't speak. He wasn't sure he heard correctly. Was his father saying that he'd loved Angelika?

"The marriage was arranged," he protested.

"Agreed to. Not arranged," Stavros said. "She was to marry someone else. Someone of her own class and background. Not a young upstart like me. A *real* Greek. Not an immigrant who left his country behind. That is what her father said." The older man shook his head. "I comfort myself sometimes thinking that it wouldn't have been any different if she'd married him. But I don't know."

"What the hell are you talking about?" None of this made any sense to Nikos. "Are you saying you took her away from another man?"

"I loved her," Stavros said simply. "She loved me. She would not marry him. She refused. She wanted me, she told her father. She wouldn't marry anyone else. Angelika could be very persuasive," he added ruefully. "I know."

Nikos knew, too. His mother had always been able to bend him to her will. Not by force but by the warmth and sweetness of her character. But that his father had *loved* her? He didn't know what to think.

"It was a wonderful marriage," Stavros went on, his voice almost dreamy all at once as he stared off into space, seeing, Nikos guessed, the early years of his life with Angelika. "We worked hard together. We played together. We loved each other. And what we had was in two years made better by the arrival of a son." Here he flickered back to the present long enough to look over at that son. "A perfect son." Stavros smiled a little sadly.

His father had thought he was perfect? Well, maybe once he had...a long, long time ago.

"I took you everywhere," he said to Nikos. "To work. To the beach. To sail. You loved to sail."

Nikos didn't remember loving to sail—not with his father anyway. He didn't recall ever sailing with his father. He remembered sitting in the boat, waiting... waiting... He must have been very small.

Yes, he did remember it now. How eager he had been. How much he had waited for the afternoon to come when his father would be back from a trip so they could go sailing again. Again? Something flickered through his mind. Vague displaced memories. The feel of the wind in his face, of the list of the boat, of his father's strong arm around his narrow shoulders. Yes, they had gone sailing...until...

"We were best friends once," Stavros continued. "And all your mother and I could think was how wonderful it would be to have more children like you. So she got pregnant again. And she lost that child. A miscarriage. These things happen, the doctor said. We tried again. And again. More miscarriages. She was in bed a lot. Do you remember? She used to read to you in her bed."

Nikos remembered. He hadn't known why she was in bed. She was "resting," she always told him.

"Come keep me company for a little while," she would say. And she would read to him.

"She needed you there," his father said. "You were the bright spot in her day. So I didn't take you with me so much anymore. Sometimes, though, I took you sailing. I remember the last time. You were five. We had planned it for a week, maybe more. I'd had to go to Athens and I was looking forward to coming home to your mother, who was expecting again, and to you. And when I got there, she was being rushed to the hospital. Another miscarriage. And of course I went with her, not to you. You never forgave me for that.'' He smiled a little. ''You wouldn't listen when I tried to explain. You ran out of the room.''

Nikos wanted to deny it. He couldn't. He remembered the waiting. He'd been waiting forever for his father to come. ''Soon,'' his mother would say. ''Soon he will come.'' And then, ''Tomorrow.'' And then, ''In a few hours.'' White-faced, she said then, ''Nikos, run get Mrs. Agnostopolis next door.'' He had.

Then he'd gone down to the dock to wait for his father.

But his father had never come.

And he hadn't listened. He'd been angry. Furious. ''You promised,'' he'd yelled. And then he'd run. He remembered it now as if it were yesterday. And he remembered, too, that he'd never gone sailing with his father again.

''I was a child,'' he said gruffly, looking away, watching as another child went limp as its mother tried to get it to walk toward the gate.

''You were a child,'' Stavros agreed. ''I should have made you listen. I thought you would come around. I had other things on my mind. Your mother. Her health. My business. It was necessary to work very hard just then. I wanted to prove to your mother's father that I was worthy of her, you see.''

Nikos wasn't sure he saw at all. But he didn't run this time. He sat still. He wanted to know. He had so many questions.

"If you loved her, why did you leave?" He tried to make his voice sound casual, as if he was inquiring about the weather. But even he could hear the anguish in it. His jaw locked. He looked away.

Stavros sighed. "Because I was a fool. 'One last time,' she said to me. 'I want to try to have a baby one last time.' You were almost eight. She wanted you to have a brother or a sister. She knew how much I wanted more children. She wanted them herself. 'Please,' she begged me. And—" he shook his head "—I said yes. Our miracle, she called it when she not only got pregnant, but *stayed* pregnant. She was very careful. *I* was very careful. I didn't go near her for fear of making her miscarry. She was doing very well. So well that I took a chance and went to Athens for a meeting. A weekend, I promised her. It was necessary for a merger. She wasn't due for two months. All was well." His voice faded. He stared at his hands which lay loosely in his lap. His shoulders sagged. He looked like a very old man.

Nikos waited for him to say it, even though he thought he knew. He remembered Julietta's words, *Poor Stavros. It'll be just like last time.* Only now Nikos understood what she meant.

"She hemorrhaged. There was something wrong with the placenta, a ridge in it or something. The baby was finally big enough and active enough to kick a piece of it loose. She went into labor the night I left. I didn't get back until after the baby was born."

"And died?" Nikos whispered. It shouldn't have been a question. He knew.

His father nodded. "Stillborn. Too small. A breech birth. She almost died. I would never have forgiven myself if she had died!" He looked at his son, and for the first time Nikos saw clearly the anguish in his father's eyes.

For a long time, neither of them spoke. Nikos tried to remember that time. He didn't remember for sure knowing that his mother was even pregnant. Surely he would have realized!

"She told you she was getting chubby, not that she was expecting a baby," Stavros said, answering the question that Nikos didn't ask. "She didn't want you to know in case it didn't happen. Now I think she was wrong. But then I said nothing. After all, she knew you better than I did."

Or thought she did, Nikos realized. His mother would have thought she was doing the right thing, not getting his hopes up, not wanting him to be disappointed. Protecting him.

"I had made plenty of mistakes up until then," Stavros went on, "but after that I made the worst of all." He folded his hands and looked straight at Nikos. His eyes were like burnt holes in his ashen face. "I still loved your mother, but I couldn't make love to her. If I did, I knew she would insist on trying again. So I stayed away from her. From you. I moved out. I thought I was protecting her. I was determined to be a martyr to my love—to do the right thing." He smiled with wry bitterness. And then his gaze dropped. "I didn't realize what I was doing by turning my back on her. I failed her. I failed you."

Beyond the glass a jet engine thrummed. Inside the terminal a loud speaker called for passengers to approach the gate. A baby cried.

And Nikos swallowed hard, blinked rapidly, and fought his own tears. He wouldn't cry. He *wouldn't!*

And he didn't, until a tear trickled down Stavros's

cheek first, and the old man reached out and pulled Nikos into his arms. Then the tears came, pressed into Stavros's shoulder as his father murmured the Greek words that Nikos had long forgotten. "Ah, my son. I love you, my son."

He was gone.

She awakened and, without even opening her eyes, Mari knew he wasn't there. The bed felt cold and empty. She felt lost.

She tried to tell herself it would be all right. *Of course it would be all right!* She would survive. Other people had survived broken hearts.

But she didn't see how.

She got up, took a shower, washed her hair, put on a fresh sundress, even made an effort with a little make-up. *Look happy, you'll feel happy,* Aunt Em always said.

Not this time, Em. Sorry, Mari thought.

But she tried. And she told herself she would have made it through the morning without crying if Alex hadn't demanded to know where Nikos was, and when she tried to say nonchalantly that he'd had to leave, Alex had burst into tears.

"He said he'd be here!" the little boy wailed. "He said if I needed him, he'd stay!"

"He was here when you needed him," Mari soothed him, pulling him into her lap and holding him close. But pressing her face against Alex's hair, rocking him in her arms, reminded her too much of Nikos—too much of what she had lost. Her tears fell, too.

And, seeing them, Alex had said fiercely, "I *hate* him!"

"No, darling, you love him," Mari said. "That's why you're so hurt."

She understood the emotion, though. She felt it herself. Hate and love all mixed up. The Costanides family ought to patent it, she thought wryly. They do it so often and so well. Now they'd done it to her, too.

She made her escape when Julietta and Georgiana came home. She let herself out the sliding door and headed across the grass toward the dunes and the beach.

It was family time, she told herself. She shouldn't intrude. A wise nanny knew when to step in—and when to step out. This was a time to step away, to let Julietta and the children bond. In a few days Stavros would be with them and they would be a family, the family he had always wanted.

Of course he wouldn't have Nikos to run his business. But she thought perhaps he had a better understanding of his older son now—even though she didn't think he knew yet that Nikos was a well-respected naval architect. He knew enough. He'd seen enough of his older son with his younger one.

Mission accomplished. More or less.

So she could leave. Soon. And the sooner the better.

She would stay for a little while because Julietta would need some help for a few weeks to get back on her feet and get her bearings. But it wouldn't be long until the other woman was capable of handling both children easily, the way she wanted to, raising them herself.

And then Mari would go.

She'd accomplished her own mission, too. She would have enough money to save her aunts' house and provide for their future, that was certain. She would get a good set of references. She was sure Stavros would provide that.

And she would have memories.

Memories of Nikos.

She dropped down just below the crest of one of the small dunes and sat, arms wrapped around her drawn up legs, and indulged herself in memories of Nikos.

The wicked grin. The plaster cast. The stubborn jaw. The dancing eyes. The faraway look. The menacing scowl. The man who had taught her the meaning of love. The man she would never forget.

The breeze blew her hair around her face. She scraped it back. It kicked up sand dervishes. It trickled down the back of her neck.

She reached up and hand and swiped at it, trying to stop it. It kept trickling. She turned—and saw a pair of bare feet. Looked up into Nikos's dark eyes. The wicked grin flashed for just an instant. Then he dropped the handful of sand he'd been pouring down her neck and squatted on the sand beside her.

She looked at him, wide-eyed, astonished. *What was he doing here?* He'd left. Gone back to Cornwall.

"The old man made me stay," he said.

She'd thought her eyes couldn't get any wider. Now they almost popped right out of her head. "What are you talking about?"

"The old man," Nikos said impatiently. "My father. Remember him?" He slanted her an ironic smile.

"What do you mean, he made you stay? Your father's in the hospital!"

"No. He tracked me down at JFK."

"What? How could he? He's under doctor's orders to—"

"I haven't met a doctor yet who could make my old man do a damn thing he didn't want to do. And in this case he was determined. I thought he was bull-headed before, trying to run my life.'' Nikos laughed wryly. ''I hadn't seen anything yet.''

Mari could barely fathom this. ''He went after you all the way to the airport? Why? To make you come back?''

''He wanted to tell me a story,'' Nikos said. The wry grin faded from his face and he settled on the sand next to her. He funneled a handful from one hand to the other, watching the flow, not her. ''Wanted to tell me about him—and my mother. About the past. About a lot of things we should have talked about a long time ago.''

Mari bit her tongue. She didn't dare say it.

Nikos said it for her. He slanted her a glance and said, ''You're entitled. Go ahead. Say *I told you so.*''

Mari shook her head wordlessly. She couldn't seem to say anything at all.

''I understand now,'' Nikos went on. He was looking at the sand again. ''I understand him.''

Mari hugged her knees a little bit tighter. The weight she'd felt lifting earlier at the very sight of him began almost imperceptibly to press down again. She tried to fight it. Told herself she ought to be glad. She *was* glad that Nikos and his father had sorted things out. She was glad he'd come to tell her, to allow her that ''I told you so'' she wouldn't say. But—

She wanted more. And she wasn't going to get it.

''He's still Stavros, though,'' Nikos went on. ''After he told me why he did what he did, he told me not to do it, too.''

Mari didn't speak. She held her breath.

''He said, 'Don't be your father's son, Nikos.''' Nikos managed a passable imitation of his father's raspy voice. '''Don't be a martyr to your love,' he said. 'You're a fool if you do.'''

He looked at her then, and Mari thought she finally

understood what it meant to have your heart in your eyes. It was the way Nikos was looking at her. He swallowed.

"I don't want to go back to Cornwall without you. I don't want to go anywhere without you. I love you. I want to marry you. And you can be damned sure," he added with a sound somewhere between a laugh and a sob, "that I'm not just saying this because my father told me to!"

She said yes.

He wouldn't have blamed her if she hadn't. He wouldn't have blamed her if she'd told him she didn't ever want to see him again.

But he was glad she hadn't.

He'd laughed and rolled her in the sand the minute she said yes, she'd marry him, and that she loved him, too.

She made him laugh a lot over the next months. She made him cry once, too.

It was the day she'd told him she was expecting their child.

"A baby?" Of course he shouldn't have been surprised. They certainly did enough of what was required for her to get in that state.

But somehow, even after taking care of Alex and Georgiana until he was an old pro at this big-brother business, Nikos had never thought of himself as a father. It made him a little nervous and oddly misty-eyed.

"You should not worry," his father said. "You will have plenty of time to worry when this baby is born and making you crazy." The old man's eyes twinkled. His color was better these days. His heart was stronger. "I want to see you be a father," he said to his oldest son.

"He wants to see me make a hash of it," Nikos grumbled to Mari.

She wrapped her arms around him, barely able to link them behind his back because her belly was so round. "I don't believe it."

"I do," Nikos muttered. But he couldn't help smiling when he thought of his father doting on three children. He could see in the old man the young man who had wanted lots of babies. He would have been good with them, Nikos thought.

Mari agreed. Then she pressed her hand to her abdomen. "And it won't be long now."

In the end, she was stronger and braver than he was; Nikos had no doubt. When he saw what Mari went through in her labor, he understood more than ever his father's pain and his mother's love.

"Never again," he told Mari fervently after, when she lay in bed, the tiny blue-swaddled bundle in her arms. "It was awful. You could have died!"

"I was fine," Mari said, holding out her free arm to him. "*You* were the one who fainted!"

"I knew it," Stavros said, coming into the room with Julietta behind him, smiling as well. Stavros went to Mari and gave her a gentle kiss. He touched the baby's cheek lightly.

Then he turned and embraced Nikos, and the two of them grinned at each other like fools. "What have I been saying? I always knew you were your father's son!"

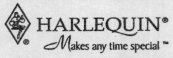

Take 2 bestselling love stories FREE

Plus get a FREE surprise gift!

Special Limited-Time Offer

Mail to Harlequin Reader Service®

**3010 Walden Avenue
P.O. Box 1867
Buffalo, N.Y. 14240-1867**

YES! Please send me 2 free Harlequin Presents® novels and my free surprise gift. Then send me 6 brand-new novels every month, which I will receive months before they appear in bookstores. Bill me at the low price of $3.12 each plus 25¢ delivery and applicable sales tax, if any*. That's the complete price, and a saving of over 10% off the cover prices—quite a bargain! I understand that accepting the books and gift places me under no obligation ever to buy any books. I can always return a shipment and cancel at any time. Even if I never buy another book from Harlequin, the 2 free books and the surprise gift are mine to keep forever.

106 HEN CH69

Name _____ (PLEASE PRINT)

Address _____ Apt. No. _____

City _____ State _____ Zip _____

This offer is limited to one order per household and not valid to present Harlequin Presents® subscribers. *Terms and prices are subject to change without notice. Sales tax applicable in N.Y.

UPRES-98   ©1990 Harlequin Enterprises Limited

Coming Next Month

HARLEQUIN PRESENTS®

THE BEST HAS JUST GOTTEN BETTER!

#2007 THE VENGEFUL HUSBAND Lynne Graham
(The Husband Hunters)
To claim her inheritance and save her home, Darcy needed a husband, *fast!* Her advertisement was answered by Gianluca Raffacani—and while *he* wasn't aware he was her child's father, *she* didn't know he wanted revenge....

#2008 THE SEXIEST MAN ALIVE Sandra Marton
(Valentine)
Finding the Sexiest Man Alive to feature in *Chic* magazine was Susannah's last hope to stop Matt Romano from taking it over. But Matt insisted on assisting her and seducing her. Was he the world's sexiest man...?

#2009 IN BED WITH THE BOSS Susan Napier
Duncan had never forgotten his one night of passion with his secretary, Kalera, even if she had. Now she was engaged to another man...and Duncan vowed to entice her back to *his* bed...for good!

#2010 EXPECTANT MISTRESS Sara Wood
(Expecting!)
Four years after their first brief affair, Adam and Trish were back together again, and she was wondering if this was another fling.... But before she could tell him she was pregnant with his baby, she received a fax from his fiancée....

#2011 ONE BRIDEGROOM REQUIRED! Sharon Kendrick
(Wanted: One Wedding Dress)
Holly had the dress; now she needed a groom! Then she met Luke who was perfect—except that he wanted an *un*consummated marriage! If Holly was to have the perfect wedding *night*, this virgin would have to seduce her husband!

#2012 A FORBIDDEN DESIRE Robyn Donald
(50th Book)
Paul McAlpine found Jacinta mesmerizing, and now they would be spending the whole summer together. But he had to resist her—after all, she was engaged to another man....